THE MISPLACED HUSBAND

The De Petras Saga, Book 1

Emily E K Murdoch

ARE YOU SIGNED UP FOR DRAGONBLADE'S BLOG?

You'll get the latest news and information on exclusive giveaways, exclusive excerpts, coming releases, sales, free books, cover reveals and more.

Check out our complete list of authors, too!

No spam, no junk. That's a promise!

Sign Up Here

www.dragonbladepublishing.com

Dearest Reader;

Thank you for your support of a small press. At Dragonblade Publishing, we strive to bring you the highest quality Historical Romance from some of the best authors in the business. Without your support, there is no 'us', so we sincerely hope you adore these stories and find some new favorite authors along the way.

Happy Reading!

CEO, Dragonblade Publishing

Additional Dragonblade books by Author Emily E K Murdoch

The De Petras Saga
The Misplaced Husband (Book 1)
The Impoverished Dowry (Book 2)
The Contrary Debutante (Book 3)
The Determined Mistress (Book 4)
The Convenient Engagement (Book 5)

The Governess Bureau Series
A Governess of Great Talents (Book 1)
A Governess of Discretion (Book 2)
A Governess of Many Languages (Book 3)
A Governess of Prodigious Skill (Book 4)
A Governess of Unusual Experience (Book 5)
A Governess of Wise Years (Book 6)

Never The Bride Series
Always the Bridesmaid (Book 1)
Always the Chaperone (Book 2)
Always the Courtesan (Book 3)
Always the Best Friend (Book 4)
Always the Wallflower (Book 5)
Always the Bluestocking (Book 6)
Always the Rival (Book 7)
Always the Matchmaker (Book 8)
Always the Widow (Book 9)
Always the Rebel (Book 10)
Always the Mistress (Book 11)
Always the Second Choice (Book 12)

The Lyon's Den Connected World
Always the Lyon Tamer

CHAPTER ONE

April 1, 1794

THE TANTALIZING SMILE Opal de Petras gave Mr. Ransome was carefully calculated to please, and she could see it performed its job magnificently.

As the spring sunlight poured through the windows of her drawing room, the hustle and bustle of the London street just beyond filtered through the glass. Opal watched as Mr. Ransome flushed, the color creeping past his cravat, up his neck, and to his cheeks.

"Why, Mr. Ransome," Opal said in a low voice as the rest of her guests chattered at the other end of the room. "If I did not know any better, I would say you are trying to seduce me."

Perfect, Opal thought to herself as the flush deepened into a shade of pink, the rather dashing and handsome Mr. Ransome not looking away. In fact, his eyes drifted a little lower, to her lips. Opal's smile broadened.

"Well, in that case, Mrs. de Petras," said Mr. Ransome in a murmur designed only for her hearing, "you will have to get to know me better."

Opal inclined her head and dropped her gaze modestly, the compliment received and understood. That was always the benefit of being a woman of more mature years than these foolish debutantes who stepped out into Society with no idea how to hold their fans or speak to gentlemen.

She had the advantage there. Past her fifth and thirtieth birthday yet still young, Opal knew precisely how to charm a gentleman, how to make him smile, how to draw his breath, how to make his stomach swoop.

Yet never before had she enjoyed the flirtatious routine as with Mr. Ransome. He truly was a master at the wit and repartee that all good Society demanded, and he was rather pleasant to look at, too. That was certainly a help.

Gentle titters echoed around the room, and Opal looked up to see that she and Mr. Ransome had rather inclined toward each other. Straightening herself on the sofa and fluttering her fan, she smiled at the man.

"Rather warm in here, is it not, Mr. Ransome?"

Though it went against her nature to treat this style of flirting with any seriousness, for the first time in seven years, Opal maintained eye contact with a gentleman. His look was seductive, and for the first time in their conversation, it was she who was flushing.

Could she be so bold? Opal had never considered herself a coquette; everyone knew her situation, or at least what they believed of her situation. She never bothered to reveal all. That was her business.

But the truth was that she was lonely. A mother of three children with no gentleman by her side, Opal was hardly past feeling the desire of being in a man's arms.

She had been good in the eyes of Society for seven years. Seven long, lonely years.

Was it not time to have a little…entertainment?

Was it not time, in truth, for her to consider taking a lover?

Opal fluttered her fan a little more vigorously, hoping her face had not colored. *Widows took lovers all the time,* she told herself. It was almost expected. She had certainly heard whispered questions as to why she had not.

And Mr. Ransome was a perfect candidate. Handsome, flirtatious, a very good dance partner, and absolutely terrible with cards. He was also seemingly unattached, though that did not prevent the jealous looks from the other ladies in the room whom she had invited for afternoon tea.

Was she brave enough to take Mr. Ransome as her lover? Opal would not have countenanced the thought even a year ago, but now…well… She wanted to be kissed, to be held, to feel…beautiful again.

"I certainly would like to know you better," Opal said, gently tapping Mr. Ransome's shoulder with her fan as another one of her guests approached them, "but I do not think Mr. Cleland would like that."

While Mr. Ransome blustered some nonsense about not wishing to upset anyone, Mr. Cleland invited himself to join them, clearly having overheard Opal's words.

Opal smiled. Mr. Cleland would certainly not appreciate her flirting so soon after the paperwork was finalized. Her solicitor was always a stickler for decorum, and his wise guidance over the last few years had been exemplary.

It was thanks to him, after all, that she had been legally declared a widow, and could now take her place in respectable Society.

It had been a good while since Opal had had any real influence over a gentleman, and she was beginning to find since she had decided this spring to re-enter Society, that it was indulgently delightful.

The way a word, a look, a mere glance could turn even the calmest of gentlemen into a quivering mess.

It was pleasing, in short, to know her talents had not disappeared after her period of loneliness.

Opal swallowed as the two men attempted to show each other just how little they cared about gaining her attention, while clearly demonstrating just how important she was to them. Mr. Ransome, she had expected, but Mr. Cleland? Evidently, there had been ulterior motives in his eagerness to assist her in being declared legally single.

It all felt rather silly, really. Flirtations, jests, lingering looks. She had known true love once. Known it and claimed it, enjoyed it for a few years before it had ended abruptly.

Now nothing else would compare. One could not enjoy ashes in one's mouth after dining on the most delectable meal.

But right now, her loneliness at a peak and her desire to be held growing with each passing year, she would take what was offered. What she demanded.

"—Mrs. de Petras, I would be honored to be even considered for your affections," Mr. Cleland offered.

Opal grinned, allowing the dimple in her cheek to appear. "I know."

There were some tuts from a trio of ladies who were standing by the window, but Opal chose to ignore them. She had endured far worse in her time. A few tuts would not dissuade her from her decision.

That was the wonderful thing about the world finally having it confirmed, officially, that one was a widow, of course. There were luxuries that a widow was permitted to get away with that a young Miss, fresh from the countryside, simply would not endure.

For example, she could take a lover.

Opal looked carefully at the two men before her, one sitting, one standing. Mr. Ransome and Mr. Cleland. Nothing particularly remarkable about either of them. Both were dressed in the finest of frock coats, splendid embroidery of blue on one and pale green on the other.

Mr. Ransome was a gentleman from trade, Mr. Cleland a gentleman through the law. Little difference lay between either.

Both were men of reputable families, but without titles, which was all to the good. Opal was no fool; if she was to take a discreet lover, it could not be with a gentleman unable himself to be discreet.

And neither man was as interesting nor exciting as…

Opal pushed the thought away. It had been seven years since Jasper de Petras had left her. Abandoned her. Disappeared in the night with goodness knows who.

The world now considered her a widow, and she had been careful to give that impression for many years. She had been alone so long that Opal had found herself sometimes believing it herself, long before the piece of paper she had been given that morning had been placed in her hands.

Now safe in her bureau, she was ready to start her new life. A new life with…

Opal smiled at Mr. Ransome as he made a particularly pertinent point, then saw Mr. Cleland flush with irritation that he had not earned one of her smiles.

Men. They were so easy to read, so easy to tease down a particular path. It was almost disappointing.

"I hope you are pleased with today's efforts, Mrs. de Petras," blustered Mr. Cleland, a bead of sweat appearing on his forehead.

Opal inclined her head. "You have been indefatigable in your efforts, Mr. Cleland, and for that I am grateful."

"A most unusual case, and one which a lesser man would not have managed," said the solicitor proudly, puffing out his chest in what he evidently considered was an impressive manner. "Husband missing—for seven years! Long enough to be declared dead, of course, but a right complicated bit of paperwork it required."

Opal smiled. *Yes, complicated.* It certainly had been difficult, but she had reached the other side now. She was a free woman.

"I suppose it would be possible," a woman from the other side of the room said in a snippy sort of voice, "to have a second cup of tea?"

Opal smiled genially. Lady Romeril was not a woman who enjoyed being outside the center of attention and had such a claim on good Society that she was surprised the woman had accepted her invitation in the first place.

"Of course, Lady Romeril," Opal said magnanimously. "I suppose you have seen a teapot before?"

It was all she could do not to laugh as she watched Lady Romeril's eyes widen. The trio of women were indeed standing by a console table with a teapot, sugar bowl, and milk jug, and it was perfectly possible for them to pour their own tea.

Opal stifled a giggle. Of course, the idea of Lady Romeril having to pour her own tea was absolutely scandalous. That was the trouble with being wealthy enough to be in the higher echelons of Society but without a title. She forgot that sometimes other people never lifted a finger for themselves.

Lady Romeril had certainly never cleaned up after one of her children or answered her own front door in haste because one of the two maids was helping Cook pluck a particularly difficult chicken.

"Pour—pour my own tea?" Lady Romeril spluttered.

Opal could see the storm brewing and decided against permitting it to occur in a teacup. Lifting the silver bell that sat on the small table beside her, she rang it.

Molly, one of the two maids of the de Petras household, appeared with a short curtsey. "M'lady?"

"Tea, Molly," Opal said succinctly, a glint in her eyes. "For my Lady Romeril. She seems unable to operate the teapot and requires some assistance."

Mr. Ransome snorted, and Mr. Cleland tried to stifle a smile but did a very poor job. Opal smiled broadly at Lady Romeril, who smiled back, though there was little warmth there.

"Why thank you, Mrs. de Petras," Lady Romeril said coolly. "I don't know what Society did without you. Do not let me disturb your fun—I believe you were about to pitch Messers Ransome and Cleland in a battle for your hand?"

The woman turned away to glare at the maid approaching her, and Opal's own gaze dropped to her hands.

Blast. That was the trouble with attempting to be clever in a spar of wits with a woman like Lady Romeril. Opal was clever, yes, though she said so herself—but she had not been bred for grand parties and intelligent conversation in English drawing rooms.

Besides, just because she was considering taking a lover, that did not mean she actually would—and it certainly did not mean that she could let her guard down.

Society was a dangerous place, and if she wanted to survive with her reputation intact, her head held high, and invitations to the very best places, she would have to do better than spatting with Lady Romeril over tea.

When one's husband disappeared—though she had never permitted that gossip to get out, of course—one had to be very careful about which friends one made, if at all.

Friends could so easily become enemies. *And enemies*, Opal thought grimly, though attempting to keep her face placid of course, *were not in short supply.*

"Tell me more about your children, Mrs. de Petras," said Mr. Cleland, drawing her from her reverie. "I so enjoyed our conversations about them when we drew up the legal petition. They are well?"

There were few things in life that could give her as much joy as her children, and merely discussing them was enough to drain away the tense knot which had been growing in her stomach at the thought of what Lady Romeril's put down may have meant for her.

"They are indeed well, I thank you," Opal said. "I have three children, Mr. Ransome, and so have been blessed three times over," she said gently, including the man in the conversation, while indicating with her fan that the solicitor should be seated.

Instead of taking the seat beside Mr. Ransome on the sofa opposite hers, Mr. Cleland rather scandalously took the seat beside her. Opal felt heat rush through her at the mere proximity of a gentleman.

She had lived in almost complete seclusion since her husband had been…misplaced.

Swallowing, Opal decided to make…delicate inquiries of both gentlemen later. Separately, of course.

"My eldest, Coral, is always attempting to care for me, much like a mother hen," Opal continued, trying not to focus on the heat of Mr. Cleland's body beside her, the very masculine scent she was now breathing doing something strange to her head. "And Micah, my son, is always in a temper."

"And your youngest?" Mr. Cleland asked, his knee perilously close to her own. "Emerald, I think you said?"

Opal's smile broadened. Was it normal for a gentleman to have such an effect on her?

"A worrier is my Emerald," Opal said, her voice a little breathless, and she looked at Mr. Ransome to distract herself, though that hardly worked. "Always looking to protect me."

"A desire I share," said Mr. Ransome softly.

Opal batted her eyelashes and looked quickly at her lap to avoid their gazes, to give herself a moment to think. Which of the two had the greater effect on her?

But she found to her great disappointment that neither touched her heart. Yes, her body responded to them. She was no fool, and after three children, she knew precisely what she wanted from them.

But she did not care for them. There was nothing in them that spoke to her heart, which was such a pity.

"I recently heard something rather scandalous about your family, Mrs. de Petras."

Lady Romeril's words, spoken clearly across the drawing room and reducing every other conversation to silence, made Opal look up hurriedly, her heart twisting painfully and missing a beat.

She had to stay calm, Opal told herself silently as she ensured to arrange her features into a smile of mild interest. The last thing she needed was to fuel more gossip.

"I couldn't possibly imagine what you mean, Lady Romeril," Opal said as sedately as she could. It was fortunate indeed that she was holding a fan, so she could tighten her grip around its delicate bone handle rather than display her concern.

Lady Romeril smirked. "Why, I have heard it is your daughter who will inherit, and not your son. Most outlandish, of course."

Gentle laughter echoed around the room. The two ladies who stood on either side of Lady Romeril, like guard dogs Opal thought most discourteously, laughed the hardest. The two gentlemen seated with Opal laughed also, as though it was a fine joke.

Opal took a deep breath, looking Lady Romeril directly in the eyes. "Yes, that is correct."

The laughter that had filled the room disappeared at once, replaced by shocked gasps from the ladies and stunned silence from the men.

In that moment, Opal wished fervently she had a close friend in London that she could depend on. Someone who would stand with her, and ensure she was not alone in these awkward situations.

As it was…

That was the trouble with being an immigrant to England at a young age, then losing one's husband so young. There was no one she could rely on, no one she could turn to in these moments and expect them to defend her.

"Goodness," said Mr. Ransome with a laugh that was a little stilted. "Was your husband not a little astonished by that decision?"

It was all Opal could do not to smile. It was difficult to recall sometimes that others did not follow her customs.

Not that anyone would ever accept them in England, she was sure. Jasper had been a man in a million to agree to them, Opal knew. Her stomach contracted slightly, and a rush of nausea threatened to overwhelm her.

She would not think of him.

"My husband agreed to those terms when we were married,"

Opal said lightly, "and in truth, it has been so long since I lost him that I have rather lived with my own rules. After all, my husband did take my name upon our marriage, sacrificing his own. Though his ship kept his name, of course. His business was his own affair."

Perhaps she should not have been so open. There were mutterings around the room now, not laughter, and she could see one of the ladies looking rather outraged.

The afternoon tea party had felt like such a wonderful idea when Opal had first conceived it. A chance to invite a few reputable people in Society, in a personal setting at home, without any of the difficulties of a dinner or a ball. A chance to gain allies in her planned ascent into Society, now she was legally a widow.

Now Opal was wondering whether she had expected far too much of people.

She had done it for her children, really. Opal had rather enjoyed her years of obscurity and quiet.

But now Coral was nearing eleven years old, Opal had come to accept that she needed to re-enter Society. If the de Petras family was going to retain its position, if Coral was to come out and be presented at Court, then Opal would need to make connections and friends, and quickly.

Only now did Opal realize just what a challenge that would be.

"Her husband took her name—so she was born a de Petras?" One of Lady Romeril's friends shook her head with a frown across her forehead. "Scandalous!"

Opal could not care less what the ladies in the room thought, but Mr. Cleland appeared to be of the same opinion. He may be her solicitor, but it appeared he did not approve of such things—an opinion she had guessed at when she had first appointed him. There was a reason she had not spilled such secrets in his office.

After a gruff cough that could have been an apology, she was not sure, the solicitor rose and strode away toward the window, muttering something about needing air.

Ah, well. It weeded out the unsuitable, she supposed.

Opal leaned forward to Mr. Ransome and whispered coquettishly, "And are you so easily afraid?"

To her great surprise and delight, Mr. Ransome winked. "Not at all. So, your daughter Coral is your heir. Most unusual. And will she keep her de Petras name when she marries?"

Nodding, relief sinking into her bones, Opal said, "I hope so, though I admit it will be difficult to find a gentleman with broad enough ideas to accept such a family tradition. Yet it is 1794, for goodness' sake! I do not think my family will be an oddity for long."

Mr. Ransome was smiling, his gaze darting to her décolletage, then back to her eyes. He reached out, taking her hand. "Oddity? That is not the word I would use to describe you."

Opal smiled teasingly. A flicker of attraction moved across her heart, but after reflection, it was only the appreciation of being admired, nothing more. It was nothing, in short, compared to what she had felt when Jasper—

But no. Opal carefully pushed the thought of him away from her mind. He had left her, abandoned her without a word, and she had managed to live as a respectable widow ever since. She was not going to let him take over her mind. He did not deserve such a place.

"Well, that is marvelous to hear," Opal said softly, her fingers curling around Mr. Ransome's hand. "Simply marvelous."

The gentleman squeezed her hand, then released it, clearly aware of propriety. Should they be seen…

But his intentions were clear. Opal breathed out slowly, as though a great tension had been released from her shoulders. The decision had been made. She would make a discreet offer of mutual enjoyment later to Mr. Ransome, and that would satiate the desires which had been building in her for some time.

And that would be that.

Lady Romeril and one of the other ladies were now standing

by the window, having a rather morbid discussion with Mr. Cleland about the situation in France.

"—simply frightening," said the woman, a quiver in her voice. "I thought this revolution of theirs was a mistake the moment I heard it, and here I am, proved right!"

"All those nobles being killed," Mr. Cleland said with a shake of his head. "Truly terrible."

"That is precisely what I think!" The woman, who Opal was almost certain was a Miss Paston, really did look pale. "And if it could happen to them—"

"I would not worry yourself, *Miss* Paston," said Lady Romeril lazily. "I do not think you have anything to fear, my dear."

Proving that even a close friendship could not protect one from Lady Romeril's acerbic tongue. Miss Paston flushed.

Opal sighed. She did like Lady Romeril, as much as one could do without wanting to throttle the woman—but goodness, it was difficult to be around her for long periods of time.

"I am sure this Terror they keep talking about is just an exaggeration," said Lady Romeril impressively, as though she had journeyed to France only yesterday to review it.

Mr. Cleland shook his head. "I am not so sure—far be it for me to disagree with you, Lady Romeril, but the French royal family themselves have been killed, murdered before the eyes of the people! If they can behead such noble blood..."

There was much exclamation from the ladies at this, and Opal shook her head wryly. Not precisely the light, entertaining topic of conversation she had hoped for at her afternoon tea.

Before she was able to introduce another, however, the door opened, and a child with flaming red hair appeared in the doorway.

"Oh, what a pretty child," a Mrs. Pullman exclaimed.

Opal smiled, her heart softening after all the snappishness it had endured from Lady Romeril. "Hello, little one."

Coral de Petras frowned. "I am not little. Emerald is the little one."

"Of course," said Opal smoothly. "What do you need, my darling?"

After glancing at the guests in the room, Coral looked back at her mother. "Cook said if you said it was allowed, we could have a little of the offcuts of the pudding she is making and—"

"You can have whatever Cook will give you," Opal said, interrupting the flow of argument that she knew would continue until she gave in. "And make sure you take Micah and Emerald with you," she added, foreseeing a disagreement immediately. "Both of them, Coral."

Her eldest pulled a face, then slipped out of the room, closing the door with a snap. Opal smiled, her heart soaring. Her husband may have been misplaced, but she had her children.

"You are a wonderful mother."

Opal looked back at Mr. Ransome and flushed with genuine pleasure for the first time. "I think you will have to ask my children about that in a few years' time to know whether I truly am! 'Tis easy to give treats today, not so easy to meter out punishment tomorrow."

Mr. Ransome nodded. "It must be difficult. On your own, as a widow, I mean."

Opal nodded. "It…it has been hard."

She had not intended to be so honest, and thoughts of Jasper were once again pushing in on her mind, but as she always had done for the last few years, she pushed them firmly away.

"One simply has to continue on as best one can."

"And you never…" Mr. Ransome hesitated as the conversation at the window continued on about France. "Did you never think about marrying again? Now that you can, I mean, take another husband? If you choose?"

A twinge of discomfort shivered up Opal's spine, and her heart quickened. This was her opportunity, she knew, and she would surely regret it if she did not take it.

Still, it was far bolder than she had ever been, and appallingly bold for a woman, even in her situation.

"No," Opal said, her breath caught in her throat. "At least, I could not even consider it until today. But I have considered…other things. Other arrangements."

Their eyes met, and a thrill of excitement rushed through her body. He understood her, she was certain. The question was, was Mr. Ransome game for such a thing? Was he interested enough in her to take her as his lover, to create a bond between them that demanded nothing of a husband and wife but pleasure?

"Other things," Mr. Ransome repeated, his gaze intense. "Well, that is good to hear. I was thinking—"

"M'lady?"

"What?" Opal snapped rather unfairly at Molly, the maid, who had stumbled into the room clearly in great haste if her untidy hair and short breaths were anything to go by.

"It's…oh, m'lady…" Molly swallowed several times, then blurted out, "The master is home!"

Silence fell in the drawing room. Opal felt every single eye affix on her.

She laughed, of course. Why, it could not be serious; it was a joke. A rather bad one, it had to be said, but then Molly was not the brightest.

"There is no master here," said Opal rather grandly, lifting her voice to ensure that all her guests could hear. "Not at the moment, anyway."

Both Mr. Ransome and Mr. Cleland laughed, and Opal relished the small victory over the situation. Lady Romeril notwithstanding, she could control *some* situations. She had managed that rather well, though she thought so herself.

Molly flushed. "But m'lady, I think you ought to—"

The door behind her slammed open, and Jasper de Petras walked in.

Chapter Two

THE THUNDERING HEART in his chest was so loud, Jasper could hardly believe it had not forced its way through his ribs and spilled out onto the floor. It was visceral, painful in its rapidity of beats. Surely the whole room could hear it.

Perhaps they could. Perhaps that was why Opal, the two gentlemen, and the ladies were staring at him in such bewilderment.

Jasper was a little disoriented. He had never lived in this house. Opal had chosen it herself after his...departure. The drawing room had vestiges of remembrance; the console table used to live in the hall in their old home, and one of the paintings, a landscape, was one he had chosen himself on their honeymoon.

But the sofas, though familiar, were upholstered with a fabric he did not recognize. There was something strange about the way his wife sat there, clearly very at home, yet in surroundings he had never seen before.

Jasper swallowed, tasting bile and fear on his tongue.

Well, here he was.

But he had managed to keep calm. At least, calm enough to knock on the door, push his way through into the hallway that was filled with delicate spring light, and tell the maid, Molly, who he was.

Not that he had needed to. He had helped hire Molly over

nine years ago, and she had recognized him immediately. At least, that was why he supposed her face had gone so pale.

"But...but...Mr. de Petras?" she had whispered, half horrified, as though he were a ghost.

It was a similar expression, now Jasper came to think of it, as the look on his wife's face.

Opal. Just as he had remembered her.

He could hardly believe that he had done it—been so bold as to storm into the room without ascertaining from Molly whether her mistress was alone. It certainly would have been a more pleasant first meeting, after all these years, if he could have spoken to Opal in private.

But he was done with hiding. Jasper had kept himself hidden for too long. Living in fear, with the terror that something awful was about to happen to the ones he loved, had taken quite a toll on him—but no longer. He was finished with that.

Jasper's eyes darted around the room, looking for the others he had come to see. Opal was there, yes, but where were the children?

They were absent. That made sense. He had not been out of polite company so long as to assume that small children would be permitted to attend an afternoon tea party, as this so clearly was.

"Dear Lord," one of the ladies muttered to the other. "Do you think that is—"

"It cannot be," said the other in reply, her eyebrows so high they were almost hidden by her fringe. "It's not possible."

Jasper was tempted to leave the room, their stares, their mutterings, and find the children. They must be here somewhere in the house—all he had to do was follow the noise...

Opal de Petras.

A slow smile crept across Jasper's face as he looked at her. He had missed her for so long that he could hardly believe that he was finally looking upon her—so beautiful, so strong, so dearly loved.

A sudden crash sounded, the clatter of china. The gentleman

standing by the window had dropped his cup of tea, liquid spilling over the rug, the saucer shattered.

"By Jove, I never thought I would see the day," he breathed.

Jasper glanced at him. What on earth had the man got himself in a twist about? Jasper had been declared legally dead—all the papers carried the announcement, and now he was here to correct it.

He turned back to Opal with a smile, hoping to catch her eye and share a smile that told him she also thought the man was being ridiculous.

But there was no smile on Opal's face. Instead of joy at his appearance, or even just pure surprise falling into delight, Jasper was astonished to see shock, and a little…was that disgust?

Surely not, Jasper told himself. He was overcome with the situation, that was all. He was not thinking clearly.

Jasper wondered whether this had been the cleverest idea after all. Perhaps he should have waited downstairs.

Now that he looked around, Jasper saw with a little distaste that the second gentleman was seated close by Opal—far too close, in his opinion. What was the blaggard doing? Did he have no idea of decorum? But then, she had been declared a widow! God, he hated the idea—despised the thought of another man… Well, he couldn't just stand here.

Jasper grinned and spread out his hands. "I am home."

Opal's mouth fell open, but still, she said nothing. The silence in the room was broken only by the delicate whispers of the ladies still staring.

"How is this possible, my dear Lady Romeril?" one of them said.

The lady she had spoken to smiled broadly. "Why, the only answer is that Mr. de Petras is not, as was previously believed…dead."

"But Mrs. de Petras is a widow!" spluttered the gentleman standing with them, clearly unable to keep his voice down. "I signed the paperwork this morning, it was approved by the highest court in the land! How can a lady be a widow if her husband is…here?"

They all stared at Jasper, whose heart contracted painfully.

Blast. He should have expected it, really, but the thought had simply not entered his head. He had not liked to think about how Opal was managing, both with the children and with daily life.

Besides, the notice of formal widowhood had only arrived at his shipyard the previous night, with the last post—but the blasted papers had been quick to share the latest gossip. He'd had no time to think, no time to plan. Just rushed to find the lodgings of his wife and then rushed over here.

He had never expected the paperwork to be finalized. For his wife to be officially…a widow.

A lady could simply not have a husband one day and no husband the next. Jasper glanced at Opal, his clever, beautiful wife. Naturally, she had needed to concoct an excuse as to why her husband was no longer living with her.

His death and her "widowhood" were certainly an explanation, but to have it declared officially?

A terrible thought struck Jasper and it winded him, making him physically gasp with the effort. Did…did that mean the children…did they believe him to be dead?

A shudder of pain passed through him, a physical reaction to the terrible thought that they may believe him gone forever.

Jasper's eyes met Opal's, and it was as though a shock of lightning passed between them. Before, it would have resulted in an embrace, a kiss, something passionate and affectionate.

This time, Opal rose hastily, mouth firmly shut. The gentleman beside her rose also and placed a hand on her shoulder, whispering something into her ear.

Rage and jealousy, the like Jasper had never known, rushed through his veins. His blood boiled as he saw the light flutter of contact between this fop and his wife, and she permitted it!

Though Jasper knew he had little right to expect it, knew that Opal had undoubtedly made friends and connections after his departure, he could not bear it.

Opal took a step toward him and hissed, "You cannot be here. You are not—Jasper!"

She had grabbed his wrist before Jasper knew what was happening and was attempting to pull him toward the door.

"*Who* is your guest, Mrs. de Petras?" The woman Jasper had heard referred to as Lady Romeril was beaming, as though Christmas had come early, and she had received the most delightful present.

"I am her—"

"Hush!" Opal said, tightening her grip most painfully on Jasper's wrist to prevent him from speaking. "Just a visitor, Lady Romeril, do not worry. He will not be staying long."

Jasper flinched. There was such visceral anger, almost venom, in his wife's tone that he was quite taken aback. Startled, he knew not what to do and was unable to prevent himself from being pulled out of the drawing room and into what appeared to be a family parlor across the hall.

This room was far less elegantly furnished, and there were toys left on a few of the seats. A small harpsichord in one corner had practice music scattered over it, and there was a small dent in one of the chairs where someone—a child—had obviously scratched it.

Jasper's heart twisted. One of his children.

Opal closed the door quietly behind them and leaned against it. Her gaze was low, focused on the rug on the floor, and though Jasper waited, she said nothing.

He waited. He owed her that, at the very least. Perhaps he should have written her a note to give her warning that he was returning; but then, the decision had been made so quickly. There had been no time to think of anything so complicated as a letter.

All these years, he had believed Opal and their children were still in Bath. Yet they had been in London. He would have to have a word with his steward, for he had been most lax in his duties.

Jasper's heart yearned to take Opal in his arms and show her, rather than try to tell her, what the absence had meant to him—but he waited. She was the head of the de Petras household, something he had agreed to when they had been married, and she needed to take the next step.

A snuffling sound. Jasper looked down and saw to his delight a large, slightly overweight, and rather tired-looking spaniel.

"Admiral!" he cried. To think, his beloved dog was still alive, after all this time!

Rushing forward, Jasper stretched out a hand to greet his pet, but he did not manage it. Admiral scampered away, just out of reach of his master. The dog leapt up onto a sofa, turned around several times, and settled down into a copper and white mass of fur.

Jasper let his hand fall foolishly to his side. "He…he doesn't know me."

"You've been gone so long," came a breathless voice. "It is natural for him to be nervous around you."

Jasper turned. His wife was still leaning against the door, cheeks still flushed.

"Nervous?"

Opal nodded, saying nothing. Jasper knew she did not need to speak—her thoughts were evident in her face.

"And the children?"

She glanced around in the direction of the room that they had just left, then sighed heavily. Without looking at him, Opal said quietly, "You cannot be here. It…it isn't possible."

It was such an unexpected reaction that Jasper responded instinctively, without considering the consequences of his words. "This is my home! Of course I should be here."

Opal looked up, and the heat of her glare was so violent, Jasper took a step backward. It was clear he had miscalculated. Just when he had been sure Opal would be delighted to welcome back her misplaced husband, he was proven quite categorically incorrect.

She was not pleased to see him. There was such ire in her

look that Jasper was surprised he was not scalded, branded by her fury.

"*Your* home?" Opal repeated, such vehemence in her words that Jasper took another step back. "Not for the last seven years—and in fact, you have never been in this house before. You should not be here, not after you disappeared! Jasper de Petras, this morning I had you legally declared dead! We are not married!"

Jasper swallowed. He knew there would be some hurt, some confusion, for theirs was a rather unusual circumstance, that was true. Husbands did not typically become misplaced.

But, surely, after reading his letter, she could understand why he had taken such a drastic step?

"I have heard nothing from you for the last seven years," said Opal quietly, taking a step toward him as though advancing an army. "Do you think, honestly, that you deserve to be able to just walk back into my life—into *our* lives—as though nothing has happened?"

He swallowed. When she put it like that…well, it was rather unreasonable. There were consequences, Opal had always said, to every decision. Right or wrong, good or bad, whatever you did, there were consequences.

Consequences one could not always predict.

Jasper examined Opal closely, and saw the pain in her eyes, the frustration in her fingers as they clenched together in fists.

As though she would quite like to pummel him into the ground.

He had been certain, and he was always certain with Opal. Always. Right from the very first moment that he had met her.

Jasper would never forget it. It had been Maltravers's choice to include Italy in their Grand Tour once they left Oxford—of course, he had not been Maltravers then; his father had still been the earl.

Jasper had not been interested. "I hear the German forests are far more spectacular," he had said.

But the future earl had insisted, and as he insisted on so few things on their journey—with Maltravers paying for most of the dratted thing—he eventually got his own way.

Which was why two English gentlemen had been found meandering through the streets of Rome one evening, dappled Italian sun lazily falling onto the cobbles. Jasper had finally admitted their sojourn to the Italian lakes had been rather spectacular, and no, he did not regret seeing Rome in the slightest—when it happened.

They turned a corner. That was all. Jasper had always imagined that when he married—if he married at all, which was quite another question—that his first meeting with his future wife would be across some ballroom, where ladies in dresses far too tight for them with more feathers in their hair than was fashionable, would stand on one side of the room and the gentlemen on the other.

But it was not to be. As Jasper and Maltravers turned the corner, there she was.

Opal.

Standing there in a delicate cotton gown in the Italian style, slightly more revealing than the English, which was all to the good, with a basket of lemons on one arm.

The love of his life.

Of course, Jasper had not known her then, but he would. He had known that he would love her. That he loved her.

Love at first sight. Jasper had believed it all nonsense, and then it had happened.

Jasper had smiled, and she had smiled back, her pretty eyes dancing over him as she inspected him in that rather endearingly direct way that Italian women had.

Though his own footsteps had failed him, and he had been unable to advance any further along the street, Maltravers staring at him as though he was possessed, Opal had walked up to him, the scent of lemons rising in the air.

"Why, good evening," she had said in perfect English, a knowing smile on her face. "And just who might you be?"

And that was it. Jasper could not remember what he had said, naturally, only that he had been able to make her laugh within minutes. Perhaps she had been amused by him. It was certainly possible.

Jasper had not cared. She had laughed.

Even now, as Opal glared with such fury, he could still recall the Italian sun raining down on them and the way Opal's eyes had shimmered with amusement, and the sense, the indefatigable sense, that Jasper had just met the most important person in the world.

The person who would fulfill him, love him, care for him, and be cared for by him for the rest of his life.

It had all felt so easy, then. Jasper had believed it would always be that easy for them. That everything would be so instinctive, so natural.

But of course, it hadn't.

He had made a decision seven years ago and not consulted Opal. He ran his own shipping business, after all, and he was merely taking a trip on one of his own ships. It did not require her involvement, and he had left her that letter. That had seemed sufficient.

Jasper had never wondered whether it was, never considered it a mistake until this very moment.

Until he looked into Opal's eyes and saw the hurt he had caused her.

Jasper swallowed and did the only thing he could think to do—reached out his hand.

Everything would be easier, it always was, if he had Opal's hand in his own. Nothing was insurmountable as long as they faced it together. Once she took it, and Jasper knew she would, then she would understand. She would see that no matter what they needed to resolve, what they must discuss, they would do it together. They had never had to explain things to each other before.

"Opal—"

She took a step back, pointedly ignoring his hand. "I need to think."

She had turned her head, so Jasper could no longer see the expression on her face, but he did not need to.

It had been too long, he thought darkly. All the instincts which made him an excellent husband, at least in Opal's opinion, had gone.

"I must get rid of everyone," said Opal distractedly, glancing at the door again.

Jasper swallowed. It was a stark reminder of just how separate he had been from her life during the years of his absence. "Friends of yours?"

Opal laughed dryly. "Oh, I wouldn't go that far."

Her response made no sense, but then, he had never been particularly good at playing all those games Society demanded. That had always been Opal's forte. It was only when he had left his family that Jasper had realized just how much of the world she navigated for him.

Opal glanced at him, clearly saw his confused face, and sighed heavily. "Look, go upstairs. First door on the left, the guest chamber. I'll ask Molly or Meredith to make up the bed for you."

"Meredith?"

"Our second maid," Opal explained.

Jasper frowned. "Our second maid is Abigail."

The moment the words were out of his mouth, Jasper knew he had made a complete fool of himself.

"I think you will find that there have been quite a few…changes here since you decided to abandon your family," Opal said in crisp tones.

Jasper did not rise to the bait. He could see now that the time for serious conversation was not now. In truth, he was rather overwhelmed. This had not been the homecoming he had expected.

"First door on the left," he repeated quietly.

Opal nodded. "The guest chamber."

Had he dreamt it, or was there a slight emphasis in her words there? Jasper could not help but be a little hurt, after all, that he was not being given the privilege of her bed, but he supposed she had the right to withhold that.

There would be an…adjustment period. For both of them. For all of them.

And when Opal invited him back into her bed, it would be all the sweeter.

"Fine," said Jasper heavily, suddenly feeling the weight of tiredness around his shoulders. "I'll go upstairs, you will get rid of your guests—and then, can we talk?"

Opal was still not looking at him, as though his mere presence caused her pain. He tried to catch her gaze, tried to see what she was thinking, but she was closed to him in a way she never had been before.

"I make it my business not to speak to strange gentlemen in the afternoons," Opal said coldly.

Jasper breathed a laugh. "Damnit, Opal, I am your husband."

"No, you are not," Opal said quietly. "Did you not hear me— I signed the papers this morning. You have been gone seven years, Jasper, you left me very little choice. For all intents and purposes…we are no longer married."

Jasper's jaw fell open. No. She had said the words before but had not taken them in. He had not quite believed it when the letter arrived at his lodgings, forwarded on from his shipyard's office. It was a mistake, an error. Opal was not going to…she would not have…

But she had. The woman he had made vows to all those years ago, the woman he loved, whose bed he had shared, who had borne his children…was no longer his wife?

Jasper sat heavily down on a chair. "You cannot be serious."

"More serious than I have ever been in my life," said Opal darkly, her eyes flashing. "You have been declared dead, Jasper. Legally, you no longer exist."

Jasper's heart was racing so rapidly, it was difficult to hear his wife over the pounding of his pulse in his ears.

No…not his wife. He glanced up again at the woman before him. It was not possible. It was a terrible mistake.

Was it one that could be swiftly undone?

"We have to rectify this," Jasper said quickly. "Today."

"I do not think it is that simple!" Opal said, swallowing with a grimace.

"It would almost be easier," said Jasper with a dry laugh, "to court you, and marry you again!"

His laughter echoed horribly around the room, and it was not joined by that of his wife. Dear God, this was a disaster. He was not married to Opal?

"Marry me again?" said Opal dryly. "You should be so lucky."

Opal de Petras was not a woman who had any trouble sharing her opinions; that was the Italian in her. Jasper had always loved that. Had hoped their children had inherited that trait, all of them.

Jasper's stomach lurched. And of course, he had no clue whether they had. Coral had been—what, six years old? Almost seven? Micah, a year younger when he had left. Their youngest had not even been born. He didn't even know the child's name.

Spurred on by these painful thoughts, Jasper stepped forward. "When can I see the children?"

Opal's gaze snapped to him. "When I decide—and I mean that, Jasper. This has been hard on them, Coral most of all, and with you here so suddenly…on this day, of all days. You…you are here to stay, aren't you?"

There was a tremor in her voice, and it softened Jasper's heart as nothing else could. There were many conversations to be had, explanations, and stories to share.

Children to meet.

"Yes," said Jasper firmly. "I will be your misplaced husband no longer. I am here to stay."

Fixing him with another stern stare, then turning to open the door, Opal said quietly, "We will see. But let's get one thing clear between us, shall we? You are not my husband."

CHAPTER THREE

April 8, 1794

EVERY BREATH WAS painful, but Opal forced herself to take another one. She had to keep going. One breath at a time. One step at a time.

One terribly awkward, excruciating, ridiculous step at a time.

"I will be your misplaced husband no longer. I am here to stay."

Her husband's—her former husband's—words rang in her ears so loudly, Opal could barely hear the niceties from her guests as she stood by the front door, gently chivying them out of the house.

"Thank you," said Miss Paston coldly, "for an interesting afternoon."

Opal forced herself to smile. Why was it that for most of the time she spent in Society, she was forcing herself to smile? One would think the whole point of going into Society was to enjoy oneself, but apparently not.

Admittedly, never before had she been forced to smile at someone who was so clearly about to spread a rumor about her. It was going to be a difficult few weeks. She would have to make a note to Mrs. Clarkson, the housekeeper, not to bring any scandal sheets into the house, in case the children saw them.

Her name would be all over them.

She was not sure how the woman had managed it, but Lady Romeril was still standing there, in her light redingote and bonnet, a broad grin across her face.

"Well," said Lady Romeril heartily.

"Well, indeed," Opal repeated, deciding not to attempt to argue with her.

Her blood was already up from dealing with Jasper. The last thing she wished to do was debate with Lady Romeril—and so publicly, too.

One never knew if the maids were listening.

"You simply must come again," Opal said politely, looking pointedly at the open front door.

Lady Romeril's smile widened, but she did not step toward it. "Oh, I certainly will if you continue to resurrect people from the dead for our entertainment. How simply marvelous. And on the day of your widowhood, too. Did you know your husband was still living?"

Opal's smile flickered, but she managed to control it. She had never met anyone quite so direct as Lady Romeril—except herself, of course. Perhaps that was why they got on so well, yet could not find the warmth in each other.

"I always aim to entertain," Opal said, placing a hand on Lady Romeril's shoulder and none-too-gently forcing her to walk forward, moving her to the front step of the house. "Yet too much excitement, as I am sure you are aware, can be too much of a good thing."

Lady Romeril's eyes sparkled. "What a way with words you have, Mrs. de Petras. And how precisely do you believe you will talk yourself out of this one?"

Opal had an answer, but it did not require words. She shut the front door in the woman's face.

Even through the heavy wood, Opal heard Lady Romeril's squeal of surprise and smiled ruefully as she shook her head. She should not have permitted her temper to get the better of her. It was not the most auspicious way to treat someone who held her reputation in the palm of her hand. Everyone knew Lady Romeril could make or break someone's position in Society.

Opal leaned against the closed door and slid very slowly to sit on the floor.

Lady Romeril, however, was not the greatest of her problems, and that said something. No, it was the reason for Lady Romeril's glee that required her full attention.

Jasper de Petras.

Opal closed her eyes. *Jasper. He was back.*

And on an unassuming Tuesday, when she had received the stamped paperwork, shaken hands with Mr. Cleland, hosted a small gathering of acquaintances, and, Opal flushed to even think it, was seriously considering taking a lover, Jasper walked back into her life. As though he had never been away.

It was infuriating. It was exhausting. It was wonderful. It was terrible.

Opal could barely capture a sense of the emotions swirling in her heart. Delight, fear, anger—frustration he had given her no warning and panic he would disappear as soon as she took her eyes from him.

Jasper was back. Back in her life, perhaps forever. Could she trust that? She had trusted him before, then he had disappeared from Bath completely.

How on earth was she supposed to navigate these storms of emotions—not only for herself but for her children? What was anyone supposed to do with a man like that?

Opal opened her eyes, and the familiar scene of the hallway swam into view. The coatrack with her redingote, and the three children's bonnets and caps. The trunk that held their winter redingotes. That awful painting of the Italian countryside Jasper had insisted on buying when they saw it in an exhibition in Bath all those years ago.

The accustomed corridor brought a little soothing to her soul, and Opal felt her shoulders relax slightly. Not everything had changed. Most of her life was the same, surely, and she would be able to continue much as she had before.

Except…she had a husband now. Again.

You do not have to take him back, a small voice whispered in her mind.

It was an intriguing thought. She had, after all, managed without him quite well over the years, and as the head of the family, Opal had access to her wealth just as if Jasper had been here. The children were…accustomed, she could say, to life without him.

And she could not trust him. That much was certain. A man did not walk out on his family with no warning, no conversation, no note of any kind, then just expect to be welcomed back with open arms.

Opal sighed heavily and closed her eyes again. Oh, the first few months…

Waking in the middle of the night, reaching out for him, then sobbing in the quiet, muffling her tears so the children would not hear her.

Answering all those awkward questions from their friends. Putting out delicate inquiries, hoping beyond hope she would find him, even visiting his shipyard, meeting with that irritating steward of his, only to hear that they had heard nothing from him either.

Facing the terrible possibilities and asking the fishermen on the river whether they had seen a body…

Opal clenched her jaw and opened her eyes. The suffering she had been through, the agony of being alone, of losing the man she loved—and to what? To another woman? For that surely could be the only reason why a man would disappear, leaving his wife and children.

No, that could not be borne.

Eventually, the whole thing had been impossible, and she had quit the Bath house, packed up their lives, and come here. To London. To the anonymity of a genteel street with no pretensions. She had no need to enter Society, no interest in making friends.

Until now.

Opal almost laughed as she rose and brushed her skirts. There was no point feeling sorry for herself. She had played that game already. Living quietly as a widow had given her time to reflect, time to strengthen, and she had never been more determined.

Until Jasper turned up unannounced.

Opal walked into the drawing room and sighed heavily. The evidence of her tea party was still there—teacups all over the place and crumbs precisely where crumbs should not be. The shattered teacup where her solicitor had dropped it, the spilled tea now soaking into the rug.

There was a card left on the sofa where she had been sitting. Opal walked over to it and picked it up, a wry smile appearing when she saw who it was from.

Mr. Ransome, esquire.

And underneath the printed name, a few words were scratched in pencil.

I will call again.

Oh, it was all so complicated. Opal had never been one for being a slave to her emotions; it had taken her seven years to even consider taking a lover, though she had missed Jasper and his kisses with a passion.

And Mr. Ransome had seemed to come into her life at precisely the right moment, when it would be easy to find a little pleasure, a little entertainment, without her heart being affected.

It was everything she had wanted…and then Jasper had returned.

What did *he* want? Opal knew he must want something, otherwise, why would he return? Seven years, a not unsubstantial time. When someone wanted a little break from one's spouse, and it did happen, even in the most refined of families, there was usually talk of a European trip, a preference for different houses, and visiting one's family.

Anything that one could say in polite company that could,

perhaps, be genuine.

If Jasper had wished for time away from her, why did he not pick one of those—*or at least talk to her,* Opal thought irritably as she slipped the card into her corset and plumped up a cushion.

Could Jasper have returned to her any moment, should he want to do so? That was what stung.

Why was he able to just walk back into her life when she had wept for him, wondered whether she had done anything wrong to deserve such abandonment?

For a moment, the reality of her situation hit Opal so hard, she was sure her legs would not hold her. Collapsing gently into a chair, she tried to think clearly, tried to stay calm.

She had to explain it to Society, though goodness knows what rumors were already scuttling about on the wings of Lady Romeril's whispers.

The quiet and respectable Mrs. de Petras, the widow, not actually a widow? It was a scandal. It would be all across Town.

It would certainly make Coral's entrance into Society rather difficult.

Opal rose unsteadily to her feet and knew she could not put it off any longer. Sitting here, hoping someone else would deal with the difficulties…that was something other ladies could do.

Opal knew waiting for the problem to solve itself was simply not reasonable.

Besides, Jasper would not stay upstairs alone for long. Unless he had experienced a dramatic change in character since she had last seen him—something that was possible, though not probable—his patience would wear thin within an hour. That was the time she had.

Steeling herself against the multiple questions that would surely be raining upon her as soon as she shared the news, Opal left the drawing room and entered the parlor and looked at her three children, brought in here by the governess after the guests had departed.

There was Coral at the harpsichord, picking out a tune absolutely terribly. She really should have lessons, adding that to the one hundred and one things she needed to sort out in the coming days. There was only so much she could teach a child when it came to music.

Micah was lying on the sofa, Admiral across his lap, the dog fast asleep. His eyes were open, staring at the ceiling. He was a child advanced in his years in petulance, something she had worked hard to keep out of him, but to no avail. There was no malice in him, of course, but he had all the irritability of a gentleman sent down from Cambridge.

And there was Emerald. Her favorite doll—at least, her favorite one of this week—was in her hands, the little girl making Betty walk along the rug by the sofa.

At the click of the door, Micah sat up, Admiral most unhappily slipping off him onto the sofa. "Mama, make Coral stop playing."

Another discordant note sounded, and Opal winced despite herself.

"Tell Micah," said Coral imperiously from the piano, continuing to play, "that I will never be any good if I do not practice."

"You'll never be any good!" shot back Micah.

Opal smiled. There was something incredible about the way a sibling got underneath one's skin. She could well remember…but the less she thought about *that*, the better.

Emerald had looked up, concern across her face already. "Don't fight!"

"Don't fight, indeed," said Opal warmly as she walked across the parlor, her skirts swishing, and stepped around an armchair to sit in it. "But as it happens, I do actually need to speak to you three. Come away from there, Coral, and come sit with me."

Coral huffed and stepped away from the harpsichord. "I'm not getting any better, Mama."

"I know, dear," Opal said in a moment of accidental honesty, "and we can talk about it another time. Up you get, Emerald."

Admiral was not moved, the children took care to sit around

the elderly dog. Her youngest crept onto the sofa beside her brother, who huffed and moved a few inches away. Opal tried not to smile. There could be nothing more irritating, she was sure, than for a boy to be surrounded by sisters.

Coral was now seated on his other side, and Opal looked at them with a despondent heart. They were so young, so innocent. Their worlds had already come crashing down, and now, here was another earthquake.

But there was nothing for it. Though her stomach twisted painfully, there was no easy way to say it. But it had to be said.

Opal took a deep breath. "Well, you know your father has been…"

And she fell at the first hurdle. It had been easier in years past never to put a name to the absence of Jasper de Petras. Naming it, somehow, would make it worse. Permanent.

"…misplaced," Opal landed on, for want of a better word. "Your father has been misplaced."

There was a puckering frown on Emerald's forehead. "Yes, we know."

Micah sighed with the irritation of a brother assured of his own intelligence, his fingers deep in Admiral's fur. "You went to the lawyer today, didn't you? You're a widow now."

A painful smile crept across Opal's face. This was all Jasper's fault. If only he had never left. Or had never come back.

"Well, he…he returned today."

The words slipped out of Opal's mouth before she could think of a more gentle way to phrase it, and perhaps that was all to the good. An immediate revelation, rather than a long and complicated explanation that the youngest would certainly not understand.

Coral's eyes were wide. "T-Truly?"

Guilt seared Opal's heart. In all this rush of confusion, it had been easy to focus on her own pain, her own regrets, her own fury.

But now she was faced, quite literally, with the pain of her children. Coral was probably the only one of the three who truly remembered him. The reality of the situation was now sinking in.

Emerald looked at her sister, then her brother, who had said nothing but was rather pale. "Mama, are you happy?"

Opal laughed dryly but quietened herself quickly. This was hardly a laughing matter, but it was such an innocent question that the girl asked.

Happy. Opal had been alone so long, she was not sure what happiness was other than what she felt with her children.

Besides, she could not fathom her emotions in this moment. She could certainly not explain them to herself, let alone another.

"He is upstairs," Opal said firmly, choosing to sidestep the question entirely. "I am going to bring him down in a few minutes to…to see you. Is that something you are happy for me to do?"

Micah shrugged, still silent, but Opal could read his expression like an open book. There was pain there, confusion, and a conflicted joy.

If only she could make it easier for them. If only she could make it easier for herself.

"Does…does this mean we are rich now?" asked Coral slowly.

Opal smiled wryly. "We were never poor, darling. Not really."

Such a worrier. Her guardian, her shadow when Jasper had first disappeared, Coral had been old enough to know something was truly wrong, but too young to really understand.

And this growing concern with money. To be sure, they had had to make some changes once Jasper disappeared. Though she had her own fortune, they had lived mainly on the income from his shipyard. With that…well.

She had not touched it. Opal had never been able to explain, even to herself, why. Perhaps a part of her thought he would claim it himself. Perhaps she thought he would use it to start his new life, wherever he was.

So, she had lived off her own income from the small number of properties she rented out. She was, after all, a woman of independent means.

When they had first met, Jasper had struggled to understand it…that sunny day in Rome, the lemon scent on the air…

Opal firmly pushed the memory aside. She could not afford to get sentimental. She could not lose herself in happy remembrances of times past when she had such a serious situation before her.

"You do not have to worry about money, little one."

Coral frowned.

"I mean, Coral," corrected Opal hastily with a smile, which was returned by her daughter.

She was going to be an interesting head of the family, Opal thought as she smiled at her eldest. Coral de Petras held the responsibility of the next generation on her shoulders, whether she understood that yet or not.

As long as Opal could guide the family through this particular scandal, of course. If not, if it proved impossible to navigate through…well, then the whole family would be ruined, and Coral's marriage prospects would be gone.

"I cannot believe it," Coral was saying quietly, almost under her breath. "Papa is back? Where has he been? Does everyone else know he is back?"

"Will everyone in London be coming here?" asked Emerald in a tremulous voice.

"Of course not," said Opal quickly. Her youngest's fear of strangers and large crowds had never been a problem while they lived in seclusion. It would need to change. "You may wish to meet a few of them, of course, but—"

"Where is he, upstairs, now?" interrupted Micah, a light in his eyes now, the conflict gone. "Can we see him?"

Opal smiled, keeping the pain inside. Micah had truly suffered, she knew, by not having his father around. It was high time for that suffering to end. "Of course. I will…I will go and get him now."

She was not able to be so swift, however. When Opal reached the top of the stairs, she found her head so dizzy that she paused there for a moment, attempting to take in the radical shift her life had taken in the last hour.

There was no better way to do this; Jasper could not hide in the house from his own children.

"Opal?"

Opal looked up. Jasper had stepped out of the guest bed-chamber with concern on his face.

"Have you told them?" he asked eagerly.

Gritting her teeth slightly and wishing she could, just for a little while longer, keep them apart, Opal knew that she could never do it. She was not the sort of woman to keep a man from his children. Even if she wanted to.

She nodded. "They are in the parlor, playing."

"I suppose Micah has his little ships going on voyages across the carpet," he said with a smile.

Opal's heart twisted. "Micah has not played with those toys for…months. Years?"

All the joy disappeared from his eyes, and guilt soared into Opal's heart for taking it.

Jasper took a step toward her. "Can I see them?"

Opal nodded again. "But you must—Jasper, wait!"

He most certainly did not wait. Heeding not her words nor her cry to halt, Jasper rushed past her, raced down the stairs, and disappeared into the parlor.

Opal sighed.

When she had descended the stairs and entered the parlor, a sight met Opal's eyes which made her stand still.

Jasper. He was standing in the middle of the room, Emerald in his arms, Coral and Micah embracing him on each side. Their eyes were closed, lost in the connection, in the embrace, and there was a glistening tear on Jasper's cheek.

The only discordant note was Admiral. The dog was resolutely still on the sofa, curled into a sleeping ball.

Opal raised a hand to her chest, her breath caught in her throat. Seeing Jasper there with her children…as if they were a family again. This was exactly what she wanted when he went missing. That was what she wanted then—but did she want it anymore?

Opal hardened her heart. She could not return to the happy marriage she had once known.

Jasper looked up, and with his free hand, reached out to her.

She hesitated. Tempting as it was to simply lose herself in Jasper's arms, to become part of this happy familial scene, the de Petras family altogether once more…

Opal could not do it.

"Come on now, children," Opal said stiffly. "It's time for dinner. You can talk to your father later."

With much reluctance, the three children let go of their father and scampered away to the kitchen.

Jasper was left in the middle of the room, his arms out-stretched. "Opal?"

Without another word, she turned away. He had lost her respect, her trust, her love.

Now he would have to earn it back.

CHAPTER FOUR

April 14, 1794

J ASPER SIGHED HAPPILY. There. It had not been difficult to find a flower seller, not in this part of London, and the red roses looked beautiful in the vase he had begged from Mrs. Clarkson, the housekeeper. Positioned in the parlor by the window, sunlight streaming through them, they looked beautiful.

Beautiful flowers for a beautiful woman.

Jasper groaned as he sat heavily on the sofa, still looking at the flowers. No, dear Lord, that was far too dull. He would have to think of something better than that.

A rose for a rose.

No, too stilted.

What married man put much thought into wooing his wife?

Jasper smiled wryly. Well, he would have to improve and fast. Though considered no longer married, he was determined to win her once again. He would have a ring on her finger—or the same ring, he was not entirely sure—before the week was out.

"What on earth are those?"

Jasper stood up hurriedly and beamed at Opal as she closed the door behind her, eyebrows raised at the offering. "Roses."

"Yes, I suppose I could have worked that out for myself," she said, far more prickly than the roses. "But why?"

It had never been this difficult, had it? It was years now, past a decade since Jasper had courted Opal de Petras. Not that it had been much of a courtship.

Love at first sight did not wait.

"Roses," said Jasper, pointing at them as his chest swelled. "For you!"

Opal looked at the bouquet, and a flicker of delight swept across her face. Then it was gone. "They are lovely."

Her words were pleasant, but her tone was icy, and Jasper's shoulders slumped a little. "I thought…well, as I am currently not your husband—"

"You are not my husband," cut in Opal, stepping across the room and picking up the vase, moving it to the harpsichord.

Jasper swallowed. "A legal technicality—but yes, I suppose so. I thought I would begin the wooing today!"

Jubilation filled his tones, but Opal merely raised an eyebrow. "Goodness."

It was rather difficult not to feel a little deflated. "I…well. I have much planned!"

"Well, I hope none of it is set in stone, for I have a busy social calendar this week," Opal said smoothly, gently chivvying Admiral off the sofa and sitting.

Jasper's mouth fell open. Busy social calendar? Her husband had just reappeared, as if from the dead, and she was worried about a few card parties?

"I don't understand."

"Your lack of understanding is the problem, Jasper," Opal said heavily, curling her feet under her. The grate was unlit, the weather unseasonably warm. "Can you not see?"

Jasper could not, but he was wise enough to keep that particular remark to himself. After all, it was not Opal's fault that she was unable to see his point of view. Her presence sparked a blaze within him, a deep desire to kiss her, which Jasper knew he could not give into. Not yet.

Not until she asked for it, and she would. She always did.

Looking out of the window rather than back at her, he watched as a raindrop slowly trickled down the pane of glass. The sunshine was fading.

"I have learned to…well," Opal said awkwardly. "Live without you."

Jasper swallowed. Of course she had, and unlike most women, she had been able to.

It was all Opal's. The house, the money, the name; she was the matriarch, the one in charge.

"You see," Opal had explained rather nervously one balmy evening in Italy when they had been able to prevent themselves from kissing for one moment, "that is the tradition in my family. The woman is the head of the household."

And Jasper had kissed her shoulder and tasted the sweet promise of pleasure to come and nodded.

"No, Jasper, listen," Opal had said, giggling slightly as she pushed him away. "I mean it. If you…if we do get married—"

"Are you trying to escape my proposal, after accepting it yesterday?" Jasper had teased, winding his fingers between hers. "I cannot believe you will abandon me so swiftly!"

"No, it's not that—it's just…well…" And Opal's gaze had fallen for a moment. "You would take my name."

It had been a rather surprising thing for her to say. Jasper had almost fallen from his seat out on Opal's terrace on one of the slopes of Rome.

"Take…take your name?"

Opal had nodded, biting her lip, clearly concerned he would respond badly. Jasper had worked to keep his face calm, even though his mind was racing.

"And it will be our eldest daughter who will inherit, not our son," Opal had said in a rush, as though now the subject was breached, she had to get everything out before she regretted it. "And her husband will take her name. In fact, all our daughters…well. They will be born a de Petras, and they'll die a de Petras. It's my way. Our way if you still want to marry me."

There had been no hesitation in Jasper's mind at that moment. He had leaned forward and kissed the lips of the woman he adored, whom he would do anything for, strange family customs be damned.

He had not minded then. It had not felt like a sacrifice, but an adventure. He was not sure whether he liked it now.

Jasper looked over at her, still curled up on the sofa. Now he was looking at her properly, without the rush of excitement fueling his nerves when he had first returned, Jasper saw not only her beauty and the strength of her character but the seven years he had missed lined on her face.

Opal had been through much. Jasper could see that now, even though it pained him and could not take back the years of anguish.

And the worst of it all, of course, was that she had done it all without him.

Taking a deep breath, Jasper thrust back his shoulders and tried to remind himself what he had vowed on that day, over ten years ago, when he had married the beautiful Opal de Petras and become her husband.

To love her. To cherish her. To honor her.

Was he doing any of these things right now, expecting her not to be upset with him? Was he acting in good faith, as a good husband, as a husband should?

No, it was patience that was called for here. If he could not be man enough to see the pain she was enduring—see it, and try to end it—what sort of a husband was he?

He may as well not even be here.

Jasper swallowed and tried to calm his stomach, which was churning with the injustice of it all. All he wanted was for things to be how they had been before he had been forced from her side.

And she should know that. Why wasn't Opal willing to see that?

"Look," said Jasper after a time. Perhaps fewer words would make him less likely to make a fool of himself. "I have missed so much of your lives—"

"Because you were entirely misplaced from our family!" Opal said, pain across her features. "That was your choice, Jasper, and we haven't even begun to talk about it. There is much I need to know, much you must tell me, but at this moment…it is too painful. I cannot hear it now."

Jasper sighed as guilt seared his heart, branded it, branded him a coward.

Opal was right, of course. She always was.

This whole situation was his fault. His damned pride. He was the one who had considered the situation and decided the best course of action was simply for him to leave, to step away from the de Petras family for their own good.

The fact that it was so blatantly the wrong decision, now he looked back, was neither here nor there.

"Did you miss us?"

"What kind of a question is that?" Jasper said, his jaw dropping. Who did she think he was?

Opal held his gaze. "A question I have to ask, Jasper. Seven years, and I heard nothing. No note, no letter, nothing. So did you miss us?"

Jasper opened his mouth, his heart pained, unsure just how he could put the agony of the separation into words. He had felt it, been dogged by it, every day. Whether on a ship or on land, arguing trade routes or counting up stock, he had felt it, a weight around his neck, around his heart. One he could barely explain.

"Yes," was all that came out. He tried to hold Opal's gaze but had to drop it. It was such a pitiful response, yet it was the truth.

Oh, it was so confusing. Jasper paced along the wall, moving to another window. The view outside was blurred by the cascading rain, the light patter increasing to a drum.

"My love for you, for all four of you…" Jasper swallowed. He had never been one to speak openly about these sorts of things, but he could see now that Opal needed that. She needed to hear it. "My love is so great that at times, it felt as though it was going to pour out of me, explode against my control because I cared so much. The agony of being apart…it was an exquisite, personal torture."

His voice cracked, and he could not continue. Only Jasper's memories of Opal had sustained him through those trying years when he had believed that staying away from her was keeping her safe.

But now they had finally suffered through those years and come together again…well. Jasper was not entirely sure whether Opal even liked him anymore.

And she had no reason to, after all.

Opal sighed heavily, and Jasper turned to look at her, eager for her to speak.

Perhaps he would not have been so eager if he had known what she was about to say.

"It is as if…as if you do not even want to accept that you are the one who caused this problem, Jasper," said Opal quietly. "This problem between us."

Jasper winced. Yes, it was a problem: the way she flinched from his touch, her refusal of entrance into her bedchamber, the way she would speak civilly to him before the children, but without a kind word.

"You are the one who disappeared," Opal pointed out.

There was no malice in her voice, not really. Jasper could discern no venom as he had felt the first day he had arrived when emotions were raw and tempers were running high.

No, there was just exhaustion. Just tiredness from having to acclimatize to his presence, which perhaps hurt Jasper the most.

"You are the one who went missing from our lives," continued Opal. "You cannot now complain that you did so when it was your actions and your actions alone which have brought us to this place."

Jasper swallowed his instinctive retort, which was not something nice to say to a lady, let alone a woman who was one's wife. Had been one's wife.

That was the trouble with the ships he had spent all his time on. They were hardly the place for a lady, though he had expected basic civility from all his men. Only now did he see that there was a lack of decorum even he hadn't realized, that had started to seep into his own conversation.

"Well," he said, "I did it to protect you."

Opal rose and moved about the room, seemingly as unable to stay in one place as he was. She moved to the bureau, a magnificent mahogany piece that Jasper had chosen himself.

Opening it, Opal removed a piece of paper and thrust it toward him. A copy of his death certificate—the same he had received.

"You cannot imagine what…what it was like. Grieving you." Opal's voice cracked, and Jasper did not allow himself to lift his gaze. He could not take in her pain, not right now. "Trying to accept that the life we had was over, that I had to continue on without you. You think I wanted to do this? Have you declared dead, our marriage over?"

Jasper swallowed. *This was not his fault.* It was that damned letter writer. If only he had been able to find out who the sender was, but all these years later, he had got absolutely nowhere with discovering the miscreant who had separated his family.

Though he wished to spend as much time with their children as possible, he was glad at this moment that they were not with them. Though that did raise the question of their location. Where were they?

Opening his mouth to ask the question, Jasper closed it hurriedly. He had no wish to look an even greater fool than he already was. Wasn't a father supposed to know where his children were? Was he such an incompetent father that—

Oh, blast. Jasper sighed. He was. How could he be a good one, as he had not been here for the majority of his children's lives?

"Where are the children?" Jasper asked weakly.

Opal looked at him with surprise. "With Miss Matilda, of course."

Jasper stared as though greater understanding would follow if he just waited patiently. Unfortunately, no matter how much he looked at her, clarity was not forthcoming.

"Miss Matilda?" he repeated.

A thin line appeared between Opal's eyes. "The governess, Jasper!"

"Well, how am I supposed to know that!" Jasper said, throwing up his hands. "I've not been here, I hardly know them!"

The words echoed around the parlor for a little too long—or perhaps they were just ringing in Jasper's own mind.

"Well, how am I supposed to know that! I've not been here, I hardly know them!"

It was a resounding indictment of his own stupidity, and Jasper could not believe the words had come from his own mouth. It was shameful. It was ridiculous. It was painful.

Worst of all, there was a smile on Opal's face that was a little too upset for his liking. "Exactly," she said crisply, her voice catching in her throat. "You hardly know them. How are you supposed to? You haven't been here, Jasper. You are nothing but a stranger to them."

Her words stung—no, it was worse than that. Jasper's chest felt as though a blade had been plunged into it, stabbing him with an agony he had never known before.

Words she could not take back.

Jasper found a tear was once again prickling in the corner of his eye, and he pushed it aside. He had missed it all—his children's accomplishments. Everything.

Time he could never get back, never retrieve.

"I still cannot believe it," he said dully. "I mean, you secured the paperwork. That I was dead."

"For all I knew, you were!" Opal said defensively, pink spots appearing on her cheeks. "And besides, I did not actually tell people until very recently! I just allowed them to…presume."

Where had this pain come from? This twisting agony across his chest, as though he was bound. He had left his family against all his wishes, to protect them from the threats that appeared, again and again, in the letters which had no signature…and she had pretended that he no longer lived?

"We had misplaced you!" Opal said with a dry laugh. "I had no idea where you were, when you were coming back—what would you do in my position?"

"I don't know."

Jasper looked again at the paper in his hands. So small, so seemingly insignificant—yet at the same time, it had unraveled an affection of over a decade, separated them formally in a way he had never expected.

"It's just a piece of paper," he said slowly. The paper was thin in his hands.

"The world is run on pieces of paper," said Opal. "Trust me, I know. The paperwork to get here…you wouldn't understand."

"But we are still married, surely," said Jasper, unable to fathom the idea that they were not. "We made vows to each other in a church."

"Until death do we part," Opal said, pain in her smile. "Yes, I remember. But by law, my dear, you are nothing to me."

Nothing to him. It was a dreadful thought, one Jasper could hardly countenance.

He would need to woo back his wife. Convince Opal he loved her, and most importantly, that she should fall in love with him again.

"You will have to allow me to accompany you to all the invitations you have accepted."

"You cannot be serious! I cannot arrive with a dead man!"

"I just do not see how me accompanying you to tea with the Romerils, seeing Maltravers, going to these balls you are invited to, is a problem!" said Jasper urgently, hoping he could persuade Opal to see his side. "Why not let me come with you?"

Why not let me become a part of your life, Jasper knew he was asking—a great boon indeed.

Opal appeared to be about to say something, but then she

hesitated. Her gaze flickered to him and then away, as though she was still getting accustomed to seeing him at all.

Which, Jasper reminded himself, she was.

"Look," said Opal quietly. "You have been here barely a week."

Jasper smiled, a true smile finally. "It feels like a lifetime."

"Well, not to me," said Opal bluntly.

Though he was tempted to speak, Jasper managed to prevent himself. The hurt on Opal's face was tangible, and he realized with a shock to his stomach that she had managed to hold most of it back these last few days.

The pain he had seen before… was only a small portion of the hurt.

Dear God, it was going to take him a while to fix this.

"This is difficult, this is all so…you were gone, Jasper." Opal sank onto a chair but did not take her gaze from him. "Gone for years. I had to learn to live without you, had to learn what a life without you looked like. I cannot just immediately bring you into it. It's going to take time."

It was a fair comment, and Jasper considered himself nothing if not a fair man. He nodded, taking a step closer, desperate to be near her. Every moment with her was a gift.

"I understand that," he said quietly.

"Do you? Because I don't think you can…the pain of losing you and knowing, at least hoping that you were somewhere safe, even if it was not with me, and not knowing…"

Her voice had become warm, open, vulnerable, but as it trailed away something changed in Opal's eyes and she drew back. It was impressive, as though a switch had been moved, and Opal's decision to be vulnerable was withdrawn.

But at that moment, Jasper had seen the genuine agony within her. It was strange, to see a person so broken because of you—because of your absence.

"I must attend Almack's tomorrow," she said. "And after that…I'll consider it. I'll consider many things."

And that appeared to be everything she had to say. Jasper waited for a moment, then nodded. "That is fair."

"And in the meantime, I will have to think what to tell people. A widow whose husband has returned…"

A cannonball sunk into Jasper's stomach as the words he had overheard when he had first arrived at the de Petras house resurfaced in his mind.

"Why, the only answer is that Mr. de Petras is not, as was previously believed…dead."

He was so close to her now that he could kiss her if he could just lean forward a few inches.

"I mean it, you know. I intend to court you." If only he could kiss her, pull her into his arms, and show her just what he had missed, what they both had missed.

A frisson of expectation shivered down Jasper's spine. He could almost taste her already, his longing so intense. Surely, she could feel it too?

Opal stepped away. "That won't solve things, Jasper, and you know it."

Jasper grinned. "It might make you feel better."

She glanced over her shoulder at him, and he saw a flicker of the old Opal. The carefree one, the one who would just as soon pin him to the bed as allow herself to be pinned.

But then it was gone. "If you cannot take this seriously—"

"Fine, fine," said Jasper, stepping away hastily and putting his hands up in mock surrender. "I just…I want you to trust me, Opal."

Perhaps it was using her name, something Jasper had not done much since his return, that did it. A sad sort of smile crept across Opal's face, and she nodded.

"I know. I want to trust you, Jasper," she said quietly. "You're just not giving me many reasons to right now."

CHAPTER FIVE

April 15, 1794

O PAL TOOK A slow, deep breath as she stood outside Almack's. Raucous noise already spilled out onto the street; the notoriously bad food, it appeared, had been avoided, and so the effects of the copious wine had already started affecting the guests' judgment.

She shivered, though the evening air was balmy. She had never enjoyed Almack's.

Not that she was a frequent visitor. Indeed, her voucher had only been offered a month ago, with the delicate and knowing smile of Lady Romeril. Without her support... Opal knew she owed the woman a debt. If only she did not take its repayment through gossip and slander...

Smoothing the light, almost opalescent blue skirts of her gown, Opal clutched her fan and strode firmly up the steps, ensuring to keep her smile in place.

That was the most important thing in Society, was it not? To always look as though one was simply having the best time? Even when one's heart was breaking...

Opal smiled at the footmen at the door, who looked surprised to have been treated with such courtesy, then smiled at the gaggle of people in the entranceway, who were muttering.

They halted, stared for a moment, then one said, "Mrs. de Petras. How interesting."

The muttered conversation continued, though this time, there were a few more glances in her direction.

It was fortunate indeed that the night air was so warm, as Opal could blame its humidity for the tinge of color undoubtedly searing her cheeks. She averted her eyes, keeping her smile fixed.

The news could not have spread that fast...could it? Surely not. And even if it had, it would be false. Lady Romeril and Miss Paston had surely misunderstood the entire situation, Opal told herself, as though merely wishing it could make it true.

Besides, nothing could be more scandalous than the truth.

Still, it was a relief to be out in the world as though nothing had changed. Opal could almost feel the tension in her shoulders dissipating. This was what Wednesday evenings had been for the last few weeks, and it was a reprieve to slip back into a semblance of routine.

A flicker of excitement seared through her heart. *Would Mr. Ransome be here?*

Immediate shame tempered the happy emotion. Her husband had returned to her, something she had considered impossible despite her constant prayers for it in the early months that he had gone missing.

Was she to sacrifice the blessing of Jasper's return for—for a mere flirtation?

Opal shivered, despite the heat of the room, as she entered the ballroom and stood to one side, the dancers taking up most of the space. No, it was altogether pleasant to get out of the house, on her own—she had been very firm with Jasper on this—and do something that did not require him nor any reconciliation with past troubles.

Here, she could relax. *Almost.*

Opal smiled and inclined her head as someone walked past, and her curtsey was returned, but there was something rather stilted about the look.

A twist of nausea crept across her stomach.

Well, news of something had certainly got out, that was clear. Opal tried not to focus on the gazes around the room turning to her, the raised eyebrows, the slight shake of the heads.

Holding her head high, Opal could not deny that as she looked around Almack's and took in the pretty gowns, the ostentatious feathers, and the rather false looking diamonds, she was looking for a friendly face.

Someone. Anyone. Even Lady Romeril was preferable to standing alone.

Only when her attention reached the punch table did she find such a person, though his face twisted her heart slightly. He had always been Jasper's friend rather than hers.

Stepping forward languidly, as though she had no particular direction to travel but thought it would be pleasant to take a turn around the room, Opal meandered slightly away from the punch table at first, her fan fluttering lazily at her side until she turned with an inclination of her head to a gaggle of people watching her and arrived right by the ladle.

"Lord Maltravers," Opal said with false brightness, curtseying to the graying gentleman with a full mustache. "How pleasant to see you this evening."

The Earl of Maltravers turned from the punch table and beamed to see her, and Opal felt the tension at the back of her neck fall away.

Jasper and Maltravers had been friends for decades—longer than she had known either of them. He had been a discreet friend of the de Petras family, helping her choose a house to purchase in London, but never straying too close to elicit gossip.

He, a widower of many years; she, more recently a widow. Until now.

"Let me help you to a glass of punch, Mrs. de Petras," said Maltravers smoothly.

Opal smiled weakly. His voice was just a little too loud to be natural. He knew, then, that the eyes of the place were on her.

What had he heard?

"Thank you," she said quietly, taking the glass and stepping slightly to the left, to permit other ladies and gentlemen to help themselves.

The earl followed her and sipped his glass. "You know, I almost thought I would not be seeing you this evening."

His voice was lower now, just a murmur, though clear enough for Opal to hear every word. Her stomach twisted, and a tingle rushed through her elbows to her fingers.

What had he heard? Had Maltravers heard the gossip—or worse, after all this time of trust, had he in fact known where Jasper was and kept the truth from her?

Opal's gaze flickered over the man's features. Older than herself by more than a decade, the Earl of Maltravers had been a steady sort in the background of her life. She had no reason to disbelieve the gentleman when he had sworn on his honor when Jasper had first disappeared, that he had no idea where the blaggard was.

But was she too trusting? Did those gray eyes belie the mischievousness of his nature, and instead conceal a liar?

"Oh, really?" she said airily, taking a sip of her punch and wishing immediately she had not done so. How was it possible to make a punch so weak yet so vinegary?

"Really," said the earl with a wry smile.

Opal attempted to return it. At least she had managed to persuade Jasper to stay at home with the children this evening, rather than accompany her to Almack's.

"It's not even possible," she had told him firstly, as Jasper had watched her carefully place her opal earbobs in her ears by the looking glass in the hallway at home. "You do not have a voucher, do not be ridiculous."

"But if you vouch for me—"

"But I don't." Opal had turned to Jasper and felt a twinge of regret at the harshness of her voice, but she could not take it back. "I don't feel as though I even know you, Jasper. How can I vouch for you before countesses and duchesses and princesses?"

She shuddered.

"Cold?"

"What?" Opal said distractedly, turning to her companion and suddenly realizing Maltravers had been speaking, but she had not taken in a word. "Cold?"

The gentleman nodded, a quizzical expression on his brow. "Yes, you shivered just then, Mrs. de Petras. Are you cold?"

Opal almost laughed. If only her problem was that simple—throw on a shawl. No, she had a far more difficult challenge ahead of her.

"Cold, at Almack's?" Opal said with a forced laugh. "Goodness, that would be the day. 'Tis always such a crush here, so many vouchers given out. I am surprised not to see my modiste."

Maltravers laughed appreciatively at her terrible joke, and Opal smiled in gratitude. That was what she needed, friendly, dull conversation with people she could trust. It was not seemly to spend her entire social life with one gentleman, of course, but here at Almack's, they could converse quite safely.

But as Maltravers launched into a description of how clever his boy was, how well he was getting on at school, Opal found herself wondering once more whether the earl knew more about Jasper's disappearance than he had let on.

Her husband had never tried to contact her—at least, Opal had never received any letters that could reasonably be considered to be from him.

But had Maltravers?

The knot of tension that accompanied all her thoughts of Jasper had returned, and with great effort, Opal tried to focus on the gentleman before her.

Then he said something that gained her attention immediately. "I heard a little rumor about you, Mrs. de Petras. Well. Not about you precisely."

Opal steeled herself for whatever might come and gripped her fan a little more tightly, as though it were a sword, prepared to defend herself. But this was not Lady Romeril or Miss Paston or another Society gossip. This was Maltravers.

She sighed heavily. "It is not a little rumor, as well you know. Please do not patronize me, Maltravers, I have enough of that in the drawing rooms and tearooms of London."

Maltravers grinned. "Sorry, Mrs. de Petras."

She smiled, despite herself. There was a reason he and Jasper had been friends for so long. "How long have you known my husband, Maltravers?"

"Goodness, too long, I would say," said the earl cheerfully. "You know how these things are, you meet a fellow and suddenly you're almost fifty."

Opal chuckled. "Then I think I am due a little of your friendship, too, Maltravers," she said, her voice dropping a little lower. "I think I may be in need of it."

"And you shall have it," he said in the same tone. "He is here, then."

"Absolutely not," Opal said with some relief.

Goodness, she could just imagine the uproar the appearance of a Mr. de Petras would cause in Almack's. A man not only without a voucher but who the best of Society had been informed was dead.

The very idea of the widowed Mrs. de Petras welcoming her husband back to life, right in the middle of Almack's…

Opal swallowed and pushed aside the idea. "No, not here, but yes, he is back with us. For the moment."

She had not intended her last few words to be so cold. Looking away from the earl, Opal sipped her disgusting punch and wondered if she could accidentally on purpose slip it into one of the potted plants dotted about the place. Quite a few of them seemed to be dying already. Perhaps they were already victims.

"Erm…actually, I meant, he is *here*, then," said Maltravers in a rather apologetic voice. "There, look."

Opal's heart stopped, then skipped an awkward beat and returned to a painful patter that seemed to echo through her whole body.

"Erm…actually, I meant, he is here, then. There, look."

It was not possible. She had been clear, perfectly clear, with Jasper that he was not to accompany her to the ball at Almack's tonight but spend the evening with the children. He had said he wanted to court her, to gain her trust. Was this how he intended to do such a thing?

Shoulders tight, fan gripped so hard Opal could see her bone through her fingers, she turned very slowly to the entrance to Almack's.

There stood an incredibly dashing man. Dressed in the best frockcoat she had ever seen, all dazzling gold embroidery and ruffles at the edges, his hair had been expertly coiffed and there was a delicate touch of rouge on his cheeks—a fancy the Court still preferred, and some of the finest gentlemen still aped.

There was a smile on his face rather akin to triumph, and he was attracting quite a significant amount of attention from the ladies near the door. Indeed, a few fluttered their feathery fans in quite a suggestive manner, a few of the mamas eyeing him for their daughters.

He was the most handsome man Opal had ever seen. It was just such a pity that he was also her husband. Had been. Oh, it was so confusing.

Jasper looked around Almack's, his gaze alighting on herself and Maltravers, and a broad grin spread across his face.

"No," breathed Opal.

Jasper strode toward them, all confidence and grace, and Opal was reminded strongly of the precise reason why she had married him. Who would not wish to be aligned with such a gentleman? To stand by his side and be admired with him? To secure his affections was to secure the greatest jewel in the world.

Opal's heart was still fluttering, but now it was a traitorous joy, a hope to have him by her side, rather than far more appropriate anger that he had defied her.

With every step he took toward her, Opal saw more heads

turning, more whispers, more gossiping, and there were snickers that made her chest tighten.

How many knew? How many had guessed?

"My word," said Maltravers awkwardly, though with a broadening smile. "My dear man. How good to see you!"

Placing his barely touched punch glass onto the table, the earl stepped forward past the frozen Opal and pulled Jasper into an embrace, clapping him on the back.

It was a brief moment before Jasper reached her, but Opal took it, grateful to compose herself. She would be mistress of herself. She would control herself, even if she wanted to rail at the man and throw him out of the place.

"I just…I want you to trust me, Opal."

"I know. I want to trust you, Jasper. You're just not giving me many reasons to right now."

The words rang in Opal's mind, hollow now though they had meant something when first spoken. Well, if that was how Jasper wanted to repay her request for trust, then Opal had no other choice but to deny him that trust.

"—so marvelous to see you," Jasper was saying as he pulled away from the earl. He grinned at Opal. "You know, I just couldn't stay away from you."

Maltravers slapped him on the arm before Opal could say a word. "Good man—let me get you a drink."

He returned to the punch table, and Jasper took advantage and walked toward Opal. Before she could do anything—berate him, glare, show him in her manner just how very displeased she was with his behavior—he did something that disarmed her completely.

He lightly kissed her forehead. "I missed you."

Opal stepped back hurriedly, almost treading on the toes of a footman, a scalding sensation on her forehead. "Not here," she hissed.

Her cheeks were now similarly hot, and Opal was sure that their color was heightened, perhaps noticeably so. Was that why that lady over there had just pointed at her?

Though the gossip rose, though Jasper had done precisely what she had begged him not to, Opal was determined, despite it all, to hold her head high.

And she did. She also took a sip of that damned punch. Anything to prevent herself from spitting poison at the man.

"Here you go!"

Opal jumped as Maltravers returned and passed Jasper a glass of the foul punch.

"You are fortunate to have him back, eh, Mrs. de Petras?" asked the earl cheerfully.

Opal glared at Jasper, who had the good grace to look a little sheepish.

As soon as it was polite, she would leave, taking him with her.

"Yes," she said in clipped tones. "Very fortunate."

Opal sighed and tried to look out at the dancing, anything to distract her. She felt the hypocrisy in her words. Just a few months ago, she would have been delighted to have Jasper back by her side, safe and sound.

"Yes, he could have been dead," said Opal lightly, as though their conversation was of little importance, "or betrayed me or been pressganged into the military, and I would never have known." She looked at Jasper at these words. "Because he never bothered to tell me."

Her words had their intended effect. Jasper dropped his gaze, a little flush rising around his cravat.

"You don't know the full story—"

"I don't want to hear it right now," Opal interrupted sharply. "And I do not wish to discuss it here."

Tears, unbidden and unwelcome, pricked at the corners of her eyes.

Opal took a deep breath and willed the tears to disappear as she smiled brightly at the now rather uncomfortable earl. "That is the trouble with having a misplaced husband, Maltravers. You miss the silence and the comfort and the support. You miss the moments you never even knew you liked. And then you find, slowly, that you can live without them. That you can find them elsewhere. And suddenly," Opal said coldly, "you find that you do not miss him at all."

It was a lie. Opal yearned for him in a way she could not put into words, longed to be taken into Jasper's arms and all her fears kissed away—but how could she permit him to do that when she could not even trust him to *not* attend a ball at Almack's?

Maltravers coughed. "Well. Right. I can see they are making a new set, why don't the two of you dance? I am sure it has been some time."

"A long time," said Jasper quietly, and before Opal could say a word, he had taken her hand and started pulling her to the set.

"Jasper! Jasper—let go!" Try as she might, Opal was not strong enough to release herself from Jasper's grasp and found herself propelled, most unwillingly, toward the group of dancers that were now standing in a line.

This was a nightmare—she could not dance with him!

Her skin tingled as she felt his grip tighten.

"All eyes are on us, Opal," Jasper muttered.

Opal stopped struggling, almost tripping over her skirts as she tried to keep up with his long strides.

"Fine," she said darkly as she reached the lines. "But this is for Coral, not you."

A puzzled expression appeared on Jasper's face. "Coral?"

He looked around, as though expecting their daughter to appear from an alcove.

Opal sighed. Had Jasper really been this foolish when she had married him? "You really haven't given a second thought to our children, have you? In a few years, we will be making preparations for Coral to come out into Society, and if you want her to be accepted, then we must be. If we are even still part of Society. If we manage to survive this scandal."

It seemed simple enough to her. Opal may not have been

born in England, but she had lived here long enough to under-stand their foolish customs, and no matter how strange she believed them, she was not about to permit her daughter to be left outside them.

Jasper opened his mouth, doubtless to say something idiotic.

Opal tried to calm her breathing. *It was just a dance.*

Stepping forward, she reached out her hands as was expected in the dance, and even through Jasper's gloves, she could feel his heat. His desire.

And now, in this dance, with the world watching—or so it seemed—Opal was forced to confront the very painful reality that now he was back, she wanted him to touch her, kiss her, caress her.

Be her husband again. The man who had been her husband.

Before Opal knew what was happening, Jasper had stepped away.

"Wh-What?" she murmured, looking around in surprise at the applause.

But of course. The dance had ended. The sensations of close-ness faded as Opal was reminded that she was standing in the middle of a crowded room, with everyone in Society watching. Watching her and Jasper.

Turning to leave, Jasper was once again too quick. He cap-tured her hand in his. "I want to show you something."

Opal sighed heavily as she wrenched her hand free but smiled politely as so many eyes were upon them. "What?"

Jasper jerked his head toward a nearby alcove, and Opal fol-lowed him into it, retrieving her fan from the cord around her hand. For some reason, the room was remarkably hot all of a sudden.

It was a perfectly normal alcove. Opal could see nothing in it that would attract attention or interest, so why on earth had Jasper—

Jasper. He had pulled Opal into his arms before she could say a word, his lips on hers, and it was coming home and passion and disaster, and Opal could not think, only feel.

The pressure of his lips, the roughness of his desire, the way his fingers pressed into her arms, keeping her captive, and yet Opal wanted to be here, losing herself in the kiss, the first kiss she had tasted in seven long years.

It was heady, her heart fluttering and her whole body tingling with pleasure as his tongue met hers. She lost all sense of place, of reason, of sanity; she pulled him closer, her hands entangled in his hair, her fan against his back, and kissed him most furiously.

Jasper. Her husband. The man she had married.

The kiss deepened. Pent-up longing and desperation poured from Opal, and Jasper moaned slightly as he tilted her chin to gain greater entrance.

Opal stepped away.

She should not have done it.

"Opal?" Jasper looked a little drunk, and it certainly could not be the punch. No one was drinking enough of it. "Opal, what is wrong?"

Opal searched desperately for the words, then said helplessly, "Everything."

Jasper was not fool enough to try to pacify her with fruitless platitudes. "I know. And I want to make things right—"

She had to laugh at that. "I told you not to come here, and you came!"

Opal had spoken in a hiss, conscious that Almack's was mere feet away from them.

A wry grin had slipped across Jasper's face. "Yes, I did. And you were pleased to see me, am I right?"

"I have to learn to trust you, to…to love you again."

"I will make you love me—"

"You cannot make anyone love you, Jasper!" Opal said with exasperation. *Really, did he think this entire thing a game?*

Jasper stared fiercely, as though ready for a fight, then his expression softened. "I know that."

"Do you?"

Silence fell between them, and Opal knew it was a silence they could not yet cross.

Laughter and the sound of the musicians striking up again poured into the alcove, and Opal glanced back at the main dancehall. They could not remain here. Who knew what gossip was already spreading.

"You fell in love with me before."

"At first sight," Opal said with a dry laugh. "I was young, then. I am older now."

"Wiser?" asked Jasper with a grin.

Opal swallowed. She certainly did not feel wiser. "Yes."

He stepped closer and Opal tried to step back, but there was a rather inconvenient wall in her way. "You can fall in love with me again."

Falling in love was not the problem, Opal thought wildly. "It'll take more than a look this time."

Her heart was still racing, astonished that one single kiss could have such an impact. But she could not think about this now. They were, in public.

"We have to go out," she said, "and pretend we are happy."

Was that a shadowy look on Jasper's face? It disappeared within a moment. "Right. Pretend we are happy. For your reputation."

"For Coral," Opal corrected sharply. "And Micah and Emerald."

The mention of their children seemed to bring Jasper to his senses. The strange look was gone now, and he proffered his arm. Opal took it, attempting not to notice just how right it felt.

"Yes, I suppose it is for the children," he said quietly. "Who knows what Society will say if we are not able to…to come to terms and wed again. Does that make them illegitimate?"

It was as though he had slapped her. Opal's breath was stolen from her lungs, her entire body stiff. Her children. Their children.

Could she step beyond her own wishes, her own confused heart, and merely marry him for their children?

They stepped out of the alcove and into the intrigued smiles of a whole gaggle of people, evidentially attempting to eavesdrop.

Opal smiled brightly. "Ah, Lady Romeril. Have you been introduced to my husband?"

CHAPTER SIX

April 24, 1794

J ASPER COULD FEEL the frustration swirl through his lungs and knew he could not permit it to exit his mouth.

It was tempting though. He had never been pushed so far beyond his endurance. It was as though they were designed to test his patience—and in a way, he supposed, they had been.

"Micah," he said slowly.

The young boy scowled. "Jasper."

Jasper gritted his teeth and swallowed the retort that he would certainly have received from his own father if he had been so rude. But he would not say it. He was not going to repeat those mistakes.

He and Opal had always said when they had first got married: the mistakes in their lines ended with them. They would not permit them to permeate to the next generation.

"Micah," he repeated. "Come on now, son. You know that was wrong."

The old spaniel looked dolefully up at the two of them. There was no reproach on his face, ever-loving—at least to the children—but Jasper had seen what had happened.

Tension sparked across his shoulder blades, but he was careful to prevent it from seeping into his expression.

When he had happened upon the two of them, Admiral trying to reach for his toy and Micah laughing, Jasper had known it was just youthful playing. The boy couldn't possibly know how painful it was for the dog to try to reach up on his hindquarters.

Micah stood before him, sullen and silent as ever. Emerald was now clinging to the dog, her arms wrapped around him, sobbing at the thought of Admiral being hurt.

Jasper tried to take a deep breath. It was not the children's fault; they had probably never been told. It was his own.

He looked at his son. Perhaps they were not so very different after all. Perhaps that was the trouble.

"Micah," he said firmly, lowering himself onto his haunches to look directly into the boy's eyes. From here, he could see the tension in his son's face, the red-rimmed eyes just seconds away from tears.

Jasper swallowed. Wasn't this supposed to get easier as they got older? For some reason, perhaps it was his memory playing tricks on him, but they all seemed more manageable when babes. Now they could talk, run, argue…

It made his conversation with Opal, the one he had not yet managed to have, all the more vital. Why he had left, why he had returned, what she had thought of his letter…it was so important for them to speak openly. To speak as they had never done before.

But he could not worry about that now. Lost in his thoughts, his children needed him, and he had spent more than enough time as an absent father.

"Micah, I saw you teasing Admiral," Jasper said softly, trying as best he could to ensure all blame was removed from his voice. Just the facts. That was what mattered. "You probably didn't know that it might hurt him to lean up so high. Did you?"

Micah held his gaze for a fraction of a second longer than Jasper had expected, then hung his head, shaking it as a tear fell. "I didn't think it would hurt him."

"It probably didn't," said Jasper hastily. The dog barked softly, putting his nose into the boy's hand, which tightened around his muzzle. "But I needed you to stop, which is why I might have shouted, and I am sorry for that. Do you understand?"

The boy nodded, not looking at his father.

"Coral, will you take Emerald to the nursey, please?"

Jasper had intended it as a kindness. Emerald would be removed from the dog, she would have a moment alone with her elder sister, and perhaps Opal would see them, give her comfort.

It was clear at once that Emerald did not take it as a kindness.

"I-I'm in trouble!" she wailed harder.

Jasper raised a hand to rub his temples. "You are not being punished, Em."

The girl did not hear him. Her piteous crying increased in volume, and Coral glared at their father, as though he had committed some terrible crime.

"Now you've done it," muttered Micah.

Jasper straightened up, entirely at a loss. How was one supposed to calm children? Sweets? Toys? Embraces and cuddles were out of the question; he had already tried that.

If only Opal were here. Not for the first time since he had returned to the de Petras house, Jasper ached for the love and support of his wife. Not his wife on paper perhaps, but on his heart. She would know how to explain this to Micah and keep Emerald happy. Why, she could probably do it with a quick look and smile, rather than the marchpane that he was likely going to have to send out for.

But Opal was not here. She had gone out visiting and had made it perfectly clear that he was not to accompany her.

Jasper had been tempted to retort back—but knew better than that. Holding his tongue was the easiest way to prove he was here for good. Time would be his other proof.

"Em, darling," Jasper said helplessly, reaching out for his youngest child.

Emerald screwed up her face, already red and stained with tears, and screamed at the top of her lungs.

"I will take her upstairs," said Coral with a sigh very much like her mother.

Now he had a moment to think. *Right. Emerald was taken care of—at least for now. Now to turn to his son.*

Micah was still staring at the floor, a faint flush on his cheeks. The boy knew he had done wrong, clearly, but he had no real desire to punish him. Not for a misunderstanding.

But it was not just guilt on the boy's face. Now Jasper took a closer look, he could see something else—something he hated to spot. *Fear.*

Jasper swallowed. His son feared him. Well, in some circles that would be something worth celebrating, but his heart rebelled against such tactics.

No child should fear either of their parents—but in truth, Jasper could not pretend that he was surprised. Micah had been just toddling about when he had left. The boy hardly knew him. Would not he have been afeared of a tall, strange man at his age?

"Micah," Jasper said slowly, lowering himself once again onto his haunches. "That was not very kind."

His son sighed. "I suppose it was not. But I did not know."

It was all Jasper could do not to smile. He certainly should not be encouraging his son to act in such a way, and he supposed he should be grateful the boy did not attempt to lie.

No carefully constructed excuse, no pretending that something else had occurred. Just a straightforward admission of ignorance. One had to admire that sort of bald-faced honesty.

"But not knowing," Jasper said carefully, "does not mean that you can tease Admiral or your younger sister. Either of your sisters," he added hastily. He had been a young boy in his time. He did not wish to give any opportunities for misunderstanding.

Micah sighed heavily. "But you don't understand, you haven't been here long enough to know how irritating they are!"

He may as well have stabbed his father in the heart for the pain Jasper felt. A sharp, twisting agony scorched into his stomach, burning his insides.

"It's your fault," said Micah suddenly, looking into the eyes of his father. "If you had not gone away, perhaps they would not be so irritating. Damn you!"

The words echoed around the parlor as would a bullet. Jasper stared at his son, his precious boy. He had held him when just an hour old. Now words like that spilled from his lips.

Jasper tightened his jaw. "Go to your bedchamber, Micah de Petras. No dinner for you. I want you to think about what you've said."

In a moment of silence, he was almost sure his son would rebel against him, argue back, perhaps even shout. But a look of sullen bitterness spread across his face, and he slunk out of the room, Admiral at his side, slamming the door behind them.

Jasper sank onto the sofa, collapsing face down and closing his eyes. *Parenting.* No one had ever warned him the damned thing would be far less enjoyable than the creation of life. Just when one thought one had a handle on the thing…

If only Opal was here. But how could she have dealt with it any better? It was an impossible situation—an impossible child.

"That went well."

Jasper opened his eyes as a dry voice spoke. Opal was standing in the doorway, leaning against the frame with a smug look on her face. She was dressed in her best clothes, a heavy bonnet covered in the latest fashion—boughs of cherries—held in her hand.

Relief, sweet relief, soared through Jasper. *She was here.*

The joy that rushed through him was softened, however, by the expression on her face, one that Jasper could not mistake.

He sat up hastily. "You…you are angry with me."

Opal sniffed. "Not angry. Not exactly."

Stepping into the room, she shut the door behind her with a snap.

Jasper swallowed his words, not really knowing what he would have said. Instead, as Opal stepped across the room and settled herself imperiously in an armchair, he was painfully reminded of that day. The day that had changed everything.

He had almost not gone through with it. Something in the back of his mind whispered that he should not take the threatening letters so seriously, yet Jasper had been overcome with fear for his family.

The family that he could not protect, other than leaving them.

It had been sunny. Warm sunshine had drifted through the windows of their Bath home as he had packed the very last item into his trunk. Closing it had been difficult; Jasper had not at that time decided where he was to go, so had attempted to take as much of both his summer and winter wardrobe as possible. He had taken money from the bureau, guilt searing his heart but knowing he must take it to survive.

How long he would be away...it had been impossible to guess. Until the danger had passed. However long that would be.

The note he had carefully written, agonizing over every single line, was placed on the side table in the hall, where all letters were placed by their maids when the post arrived.

At least, Jasper had comforted himself as he had stood there in the silent house, Opal would know why he had done this. Why he had been driven to take such drastic action. Why he had made the decision to leave.

Not that it had been a decision, not really. Not after someone had threatened him, threatened Opal, their children. The whole family.

Jasper swallowed hard and pulled back into the present as Opal cleared her throat pointedly. He could not permit his feelings to show, not after he had done so much to protect them from that potential pain.

There was a sad sort of wistfulness on Opal's face, and Jasper's stomach lurched. This distance between them, this misunderstanding...all could be undone if he could explain everything to her, his full account of why he had left. How else could she begin to heal from the pain?

"I…" Jasper swallowed. *Damnit, Opal always had this effect on him.* "I know I said I was going to court you, but before that, I have to say—"

The door behind him opened, and Opal's gaze instantly drifted away.

"Yes?"

"Mr. King to see you, mistress," came the quiet voice of one of their maids.

Mr. King? Who the devil was—

A tall, well-featured man dressed in the absolute best of fashions strode into the room with his gaze affixed on Opal. Only when he had bowed to her, raised her hand to his lips, and kissed it, did he appear to notice she was not alone.

"Ah, sorry old chap," Mr. King said breezily. "Did not see you there."

Jasper stared first at him, then at Opal—an Opal who appeared to have finally lost her equilibrium. Her cheeks were stained scarlet, her gaze refusing to meet his own.

Guilt.

Fierce anger rushed through Jasper's body. What—had she been courted by this man, this Mr. King, whatever his name was? Was he wooing her, hoping to gain her affections—worse, had she…had she given herself to him?

Rage followed the anger, but Jasper attempted to force it down. It was not uncommon for widows to do such a thing, he knew, and Opal had been pretending to be a widow. Few would have blamed her if she truly had been without a husband.

Unsure precisely what he was doing, Jasper rose from his seat and stepped toward the man, who took a step back.

"Sadly, now is not particularly a good time," Opal said hastily to her guest. "Why don't you go and come again another—"

"No, no, stay, Mr. King, was it?" said Jasper breezily, his words belying the anger within.

Mr. King looked between them uncomfortably. "Yes, Mr. King, a friend of Mrs. de Petras. And…and you are, sir?"

Jasper smiled broadly. "Her husband."

"Jasper, there is no need to be so rude!" Opal said in a hiss while Mr. King looked genuinely astonished. "And you are not my husband!"

"Like hell, I'm not," he growled.

"Her…ah," Mr. King said slowly, a flicker of discomfort on his face. "Well, that…that changes things a little, Mrs. de Petras."

"I thought it would," said Jasper, his smile broadening just as his irritation blossomed. *First Micah, then Opal, and now this brute!* "Thank you for calling, Mr. King."

Stepping smartly past him and opening the door, Jasper grinned inanely at the man until he stepped through it. Then Jasper slammed the door and looked at Opal.

His breathing was rather jagged, something he only noticed now, and he was not sure how he was going to control himself.

The thought of anyone else touching Opal—she may be the matriarch of the family, but he was still her husband.

"You cannot just upend my life," Opal said curtly with a glare.

Jasper almost growled. "I am your husband. I can do precisely that if I wish."

But she was not cowed by his ill-temper. No, she laughed. Rising, Opal stepped toward him, eyes fierce.

"You are not my husband! You disappeared for years on end!" Opal pointed a finger. "Look!"

Stepping away from him, she moved to the bureau, rummaged around in it for a moment, then pulled out a newspaper. Jasper stared at it. What on earth could this be?

"Here," she said, forcing it into his hands. "See!"

Jasper looked down at the newspaper. Why on earth she thought he would want to…

His heart stopped. It started again most painfully, every beat twisting his chest.

It was his obituary.

Jasper de Petras, born Jasper Barnes, declared dead today, April

1, 1794, after being misplaced by his family for seven years. A man in his prime, it was the great shock and surprise of his family friends that Mr. de Petras disappeared and despite many efforts to locate him, it has been judged likely that he is deceased. The owner of a shipyard that transported goods across Europe and even to the tips of Africa, Mr. de Petras is survived by his widow and their three children.

Jasper swallowed. It was almost worse than the death certificate. Seeing his entire life summed up in a few lines...nothing about his wit, his passions, his friendship. Nothing that truly described him...printed there in black ink on smudged white paper...

"We joked about writing our obituaries once, do you remember?"

Jasper looked up, hardly able to think, to see Opal smiling wryly. "When we had just been married. We...we talked about all the places we would go, the children we would have, the great salon you would host."

She nodded. "I never thought I would actually have to write yours. Not...not yet."

He swallowed. It had just been a jest, a joke between them. He could well remember it, lying there on the blanket in their garden in Bath. The sun had shone, and they could not imagine a world without each other.

He was not smiling now.

"I cannot believe it," Jasper breathed, but then his chest tightened. "And I suppose this Mr. King of yours saw this and thought you were...available."

The very thought turned his stomach. His wife...well, to him at least, his wife, available to other men?

"Well, do not be surprised if I have...have missed certain things, Jasper, and considered finding them elsewhere!"

If he had thought himself astonished before, it was nothing to how he felt now. Blood boiling, heart thundering, Jasper found himself rather uncomfortably...aroused.

She had missed him. She had missed his touch. *Considered finding them elsewhere?*

Closing the gap, Jasper said quietly, "Well, I have missed certain things, too, and I think it's high time we made up for that!"

It did not take much to pull Opal into his arms, to place his lips on hers, and to taste the glory of her touch.

For a moment, a heart-stopping instant, it was just like old times. Wrapped together, their breath intermingled, the whole world centered on their embrace.

Then Opal pushed him away. "It is not that easy."

"It could be."

She looked at him, still in his arms, still part of him, and Jasper knew it was all coming together, just as he knew it would.

"We cannot continue like this for long," he said softly. "You need to make a decision, and soon. If Lady Romeril hasn't spread it across London—"

"You can be sure she has."

"Then our children need to be protected," Jasper said urgently. "We need to marry again, declare me alive, whatever it takes to be together!"

For a moment, he was certain she would agree—sure she understood. His heart leapt at the idea of once again being together, as they should.

"Tomorrow," Opal whispered, her eyes on his, "when I am calmer, when I have had time to sleep…tomorrow, I need to hear it."

Jasper swallowed. "It?"

She raised an eyebrow. "It. What you have been doing these last seven years. You need to tell me everything."

Jasper released her and sighed heavily. "Yes, I do. A conversation that is long overdue."

But before he left the room, he bowed his head and captured once again those teasing lips—lips he longed for.

CHAPTER SEVEN

April 25, 1794

A s Opal slowly descended the staircase the following day, it was clear something powerful had changed within her. Something felt...different. Something strange. Something she could not put her finger on.

After being the only adult in the de Petras family for such a long time, Jasper's reappearance had rather put her off-kilter, but she had thought she had adapted to that.

But no. This was different.

"Tomorrow, when I am calmer, when I have had time to sleep...tomorrow, I need to hear it."

"It?"

"It. What you have been doing these last seven years. You need to tell me everything."

"Yes, I do. A conversation that is long overdue."

Opal swallowed as she reached the bottom of the staircase and she hesitated, waiting there as though she had arranged to meet him.

Which she hadn't, of course. She had not exchanged a single word with the man after that final kiss. Jasper had not joined her for supper, and as the children had all eaten earlier, Opal had dined alone.

She was accustomed to dining alone. She had felt lonely at first, naturally, but over time she had started to relish the opportunity without the constant demands of children and running a household.

But yesterday…yesterday had been different. She had missed Jasper's company.

Opal took a deep breath. It was guilt, that was all. She should not have acted so carelessly with Mr. King when he had been announced. She should certainly not have permitted Jasper to kiss her, to regain hope so quickly that she could forgive him, move past his nonsense, and remarry him within the month!

But today was a new day. Stepping forward, Opal opened the door into the breakfast room and stiffened. Jasper was seated there.

"Good morning," Jasper said quietly, laying down his knife halfway through buttering a piece of toast. "You look lovely. Blue always suited you."

Opal stared. He had always said that. When she had cried, that time they had been invited to a dinner just before her first confinement, saying that nothing fit her and nothing suited her, what had he said?

"Everything suits you," Jasper had whispered, his arms around her in their bedchamber in Bath. "But you suit blue. Wear the blue gown."

Jasper laughed gently. "My word, it does me good to see you confused once in a while."

A smile crept across Opal's mouth, unbidden yet unrestrained. Yes, she supposed it was good to be surprised, truly, every now and again. At least, on small occasions like this. She was not sure her heart could bear another vanishing act from the man she had taken as her husband all those years ago.

"Come on in," said Jasper gently.

That was always the trouble, Opal thought as she stepped in and closed the door. Jasper always had that…that way of speaking to her. As though whispering to a horse, gently encouraging it to do what you wanted.

She did love him.

Jasper glanced at the maid who hovered at the sideboard, making sure the breakfast things were still hot. "That will be all, thank you, Molly."

Bobbing a curtsey, Molly put down the serving forks and slipped out into the hallway, leaving them alone.

Taking a deep breath, Opal took a hesitant step forward but found she could not entirely reach the table. Not yet. Not without knowing precisely what this conversation was.

Stirring herself forward, Opal reached for a chair by the table, opposite Jasper, and pulled it out, and sat.

"I...I am not sure I am prepared to hear the full tale, but I know I must," she said weakly.

"Nonsense," said Jasper cheerfully, shaking his head as he picked up the teapot and poured it into a cup for her. "You are more than ready for it. You're certainly due the truth."

He placed a slice of lemon at the side, just how she liked it. Opal's heart pattered strangely. He still remembered how she liked her tea. With the lemons that had surrounded her home when she had been a child.

Damn it all, Opal thought wryly. It would be so much easier to speak to this man if he were not so endearing.

"I was wrong."

Opal blinked. Had she really heard those words come out of Jasper's mouth?

Feeling the blaze of his gaze like a furnace, she leaned forward and picked up her tea. It was scalding, yes, but nothing like the temperature of Jasper's expression.

"I was wrong to treat you like that yesterday," said Jasper quietly, genuine contrition in his words. "Wrong to snap at your friend—"

"Acquaintance." She did not want Jasper to have an incorrect view of the matter.

At least, the matter as it currently stood. If Jasper had returned home a few days later…

"Still. He was a guest, a guest in your home," said Jasper heavily. "I should not have spoken so hastily."

Opal swallowed a scalding mouthful of tea and said nothing. Why did her heart ache so hearing those words on his lips? *Your home.* Not our home, but her home.

"Just because I have the fortune," Opal could remember saying to him in happier, more joyful times, "that does not mean this is not our home."

She said nothing but sipped more tea. What could she say? Whenever she found herself in Jasper's presence, particularly when it was the two of them alone, she was overcome with longing for what could have been. Longing to be touched by him. So why did she flee him at every opportunity?

"I was wrong," said Jasper again. "I am sorry. I love you."

Opal could not help but smile at that. "Was that not the advice the Earl of Maltravers gave you on our wedding day? The words that will always keep your wife happy?"

Jasper laughed with a rueful shake of his head. "Ah, if only it was that easy."

His dark eyes found hers, and Opal melted right there at the table. It was foolish of her, but then what woman could help it?

He was a handsome man, a charming one at that. There was a reason why she had married him so quickly—fear had struck her heart when she had seen how other ladies had fawned over him, and she had panicked. Panicked she would lose him.

But she could not permit herself to simply fall apart just because a handsome man was before her.

"I admit, I am glad to start finding a rhythm to our lives," Jasper said quietly. "Our family's life. You all mean so much to me, Opal. I could not have survived the last few years without knowing you were all well—and safe."

Opal's heart twisted. Was that not all that she had wanted, for him, for herself? That they could be a family together, all five of them. After all the time apart, she now had a chance at that—a chance fate had thrown in her direction. And she was pushing him away. Why? Because he had hurt her?

"I said I would explain everything."

Opal's gaze sharpened.

Jasper put up his hands in mock surrender. "Do not worry, there is nothing in my tale to fear. I merely wished to reiterate that I...I should not force you to move quicker than you are comfortable. In truth, I think the children have managed this whole situation better than either of us."

Opal sighed and nodded. "Agreed."

They fell into companionable silence for a while. Jasper returned to buttering his toast, and Opal sipped her tea.

The children were out with their governess, and she had no visiting planned for that morning. Would there be a better chance than this? And he had been patient. At least, Opal thought with a smile, as patient as a man was ever going to be.

She took a deep breath and said the words she knew she must say. "Look, Jasper."

"Yes?" he said quickly, dropping his toast to his plate.

Opal tried not to laugh. This was a serious moment, and she should at least attempt to treat it that way. "Do not get too excited, I am not about to propose we marry again. It is still...I am still mightily upset that you went missing."

"I know," Jasper said quietly. "And I—"

She raised a hand, knowing she could not continue if continuously interrupted—a habit he clearly had not yet managed to break. Jasper nodded, clasping his hands before him on the table. He was ready to sit and listen, a minor miracle.

Now all Opal had to do was think of what to say.

"You...you hurt me deeply, Jasper," she said bluntly. "More deeply, I think, than you can possibly know. The idea of just stepping into our marriage again, even for the sake of the children...I cannot do it immediately. I must write to Mr. Cleland."

Why did it hurt so much to be this vulnerable? Opal could

feel her heart growing heavier with each word she said as the pain she had buried for so long was brought to the surface.

But it was impossible not to speak. Not now she was sure, almost certain, that Jasper truly wished to make amends. To make this marriage, such that it was, work.

"Because I want to…I want to heal," admitted Opal wistfully, smiling slightly as she caught Jasper's gaze. "I want to heal this family, find a way to be together again, whole, not just in body but in spirit. We…we cannot go on like this."

Jasper nodded eagerly. He really did adore her. There was something so intensively flattering about being adored. One could get used to it.

Opal sighed, then tried to bring briskness to her voice. "Well then. Let us talk about it. You left seven years ago, and you returned last month. Why?"

Jasper unclasped his hands. Opal instinctively removed her own from the table, certain he was about to take her hands in his, but to her surprise—and slight disappointment—he did not reach for her.

Instead, he reached into his waistcoat pocket and removed what appeared to be a bundle of letters.

"Here," Jasper said quietly.

With slightly shaking hands, Opal reached out for the letters. Letters which she was sure would contain secrets, secrets hidden from her, purposefully, for years.

But when she unfolded them, placing them one after another on the table, it was to see to her surprise that they were not correspondence as such…but threats. In large, sprawling letters, Opal read:

Leave your whore wife, or we will kill her.

She picked up another.

Your children are not your own, and you had better abandon them now.

A third was just as repellent.

We could have taken your son today. Leave your family, or we will do worse tomorrow.

Opal saw rage in Jasper's eyes, his gaze was firmly set on the papers between them. She pulled out another.

Opal the whore deserves the terror in France, and unless you depart from your family, we will kidnap her and take her back there. Death to de Petras.

Opal swallowed. It was worse than she could have ever imagined. Who could hate her so entirely as to send such vile missives?

"This is ridiculous," she found herself saying. "For a start, I am Italian!"

Jasper sighed and shook his head, fingers poking at the letters as though unable to let them rest. "You think that matters to these people? You think they care? Von Bachmann, de Choiseul-Stainville, the Comte de Custine, all nobles in France who believed themselves protected, yet all went to the gallows."

Opal looked at the letters once more. Over and over again, the hatred, the vitriol towards her and her family. And the demands that Jasper leave them. Why? Who could have done such a thing?

"There was absolutely no chance that I was going to risk it," said Jasper quietly, and Opal saw the pain in his eyes. "Lose you? Lose the children, merely because I could not bear to leave you?"

"But this is a trick, surely, a jest, a terrible prank!" Opal said, hardly able to believe that anyone, let alone someone she knew, could write such things.

Jasper's hand clenched on the breakfast table. "The day I started receiving the letters, my offices at the shipyard were burgled. Ransacked, though nothing taken. Three days later, it was destroyed, glass everywhere."

Opal stared. "No."

"You think I would let those people do anything to you—to our children?" Jasper's voice was tight, pained, angry.

"They would never touch children, surely!"

"And if they did?"

She swallowed. It had been such a terrible time, only a few

years ago now, but how quickly the mind attempted to push such things away. French families in Bath disappearing overnight—no news, no warning, just an empty house. No sign of a struggle, their belongings left behind.

Gone without a trace.

She had always hoped they had gone into hiding, that they had been safe, and emerged with different names in new places. Whole communities were destroyed, and as a newcomer to England, she had wondered at the time what could happen next. Who might be next?

It had been frightening, yes, but wholly unconnected to them…at least, that was what Opal had thought. Now, with these letters before her…

Well, she had never connected what was happening in France to her misplaced husband.

She sighed heavily. "So…so you left because you thought you were protecting us."

Jasper stared with such disbelief on his face, that Opal almost wished she could retract her words immediately. "Of course I— do you think I would ever leave you of my own free will? I love you, Opal, have loved you, always will. The idea of something happening to you, our children…"

He was unable to continue, and Opal did not blame him. It was indeed a terrifying thought, one that chilled her blood. Jasper was genuinely affected. There was no way to falsify that terror. But it still did not explain why someone chose to write such horrendous letters.

"How many of these came?"

Jasper sighed. "I kept almost all of them—I admit, the first few I burned, I thought them nothing but jealous neighbors. But as they kept coming, my steward said some were being delivered to my ships—"

"Your ships?"

He nodded. "And so, I decided you were safer without me— that was what the letter writer wanted, wasn't it? I thought I could easily return home, and so I voyaged on my ships, working as a hand on some, as the ledger writer on others, and each time I came to port, there were more letters."

Opal's heart twisted. "More letters?"

"Until a year ago," said Jasper heavily. "I stayed in London, waiting, desperately unsure whether you were safe...until the papers arrived. Papers that said I was to be declared dead."

Color tinged her cheeks. "Ah. I sent them to the shipyard as a formality, I had overseen the accounts since you...since you disappeared."

Yet, he had been there, or on the ships, this entire time. Well, Opal was certainly going to have a conversation with that steward of his. He might have mentioned her husband was still alive!

"I cannot believe it," she breathed. "I wrote to your steward, the foreman, all three of your captains!"

"And I told them to lie," Jasper said sadly. "I know you, Opal. I knew you wouldn't stay away if I told you, that you would be in that shipyard before a week was out."

"Of course I would!"

"So you understand why I forced them into falsehoods," he said over her retorts. "Opal, I could not let you risk yourself—risk the children?"

"But it doesn't explain why I—why we were targeted," Opal said slowly, taking a sip of her tea, enjoying the flavor without the scalding heat. "Anyone who spent more than five minutes with me would know I was Italian."

Her accent had disappeared of course, far quicker than she expected, but still.

"Who can guess," Jasper said. "Someone jealous of us, perhaps? Jealous of our marriage?"

Opal's stomach lurched so horribly, she believed for a moment that the tea she had just swallowed was about to make a reappearance on the breakfast table.

No. No, surely not. He would not—would he?

It had all been so long ago, she had thought it was forgotten. But some people could hold a grudge far longer than she believed possible. Was it possible that after all that time, he was finally starting to punish her for her happiness?

Opal looked at Jasper and saw a smile across his face that lessened the tension within her.

"Our family is a little…unusual," Jasper said gently.

She had to laugh. "Yes. Well, if I had known…If I had known that you were trying to protect us, that you were only doing this for our good, that nothing had happened to you…"

She could not continue. Opal had struggled against it the moment the thoughts had first entered her mind, the idea that Jasper had left her for another woman.

"But you did know." Jasper's words cut across her thoughts, making her look up as he continued, "You had my note."

He spoke so easily and calmly that, for a moment, she could not take in his words.

"You had my note."

Then she blinked. "Note?"

Jasper's eyes were dazed with confusion. "I left a note—a letter, really, explaining it all. In great detail, for I spent much time on it. You mean to tell me…"

Opal's chest tightened as she tried to take a breath, as she tried to take it in. "There was no note."

"No note?" Jasper's face had fallen. "So…so you had no idea I had come to London? To the ships, that I was traveling abroad? That I was staying away only because we were threatened with death if I stayed with you? That…that I loved you, and only this dire threat could take me from you?"

Opal shook her head, trying not to think about the day she had returned home with the children to find him gone.

Jasper, gone. The man she loved beyond anything. And not just for the day or for the night. His trunk was gone. The trunk he had purchased for their honeymoon.

She had gone into labor that day, the shock forcing Emerald

from her body. She had never told him that. Perhaps she never would.

"No, no note."

"And to think this whole time," he said dully, "I thought you at least had an idea that I was protecting you. No wonder you were so furious at me when I first arrived! Whatever happened to the letter?"

She didn't know and could only shrug. It was easy to believe him, easy to trust the emotions she was seeing were true. But it was also hard. Hard to believe he could slip away so easily from their lives—but then, if she had been the recipient of these letters…

She looked at the letters. If Jasper was telling the truth, and he had not fabricated these letters, then who on earth would wish her such ill?

And if it was who she thought it was, would she ever be rid of him?

CHAPTER EIGHT

April 30, 1794

JASPER'S BOOTS FELT rather uncomfortable. *Blast.* It was too late to go back and change, wasn't it?

"Stop shifting your feet," Opal muttered.

It was all Jasper could do not to point out that she appeared to be just as nervous as he was, but he wisely held his tongue. This was not a moment to start pointing fingers. Not after they had come so far.

Still, he was certain these boots were now two sizes too small.

"And you are absolutely sure about this?" he muttered, unable to help himself.

"If you ask me that one more time," Opal said lightly, "I will start to think *you* are the one not sure about this. And you did beg to come."

A dry laugh escaped Jasper's lips, but he stopped himself from saying anything as they waited on the doorstep.

She was completely right, of course, but he was not going to tell her that. Opal had been proven right far too many times to start admitting it to her face. He was nervous. It had felt important to accompany her on these sorts of things when she had forbidden him before.

But now that he was allowed to come with her…

Well. When was the last time that he had actually gone to dinner with someone, in company? Not a hasty pie on a street corner, not a quick meal on deck, the end of a stew pot that they would not have given to a starving pig in a strange foreign town…

A formal dinner?

Tonight, they would not just be having dinner with some of Opal's acquaintances. If only it were that simple. No, the invitation had been gilded—and not a wedding invitation, which had astonished him—and was from someone with a title.

A title! Jasper shook his head wryly as they waited to be permitted entrance.

"Have I told you how beautiful you look?"

"Four times today, at the last count," Opal said, and Jasper felt his stomach jolt as her smile met his. "You are taking this wooing thing rather seriously, aren't you?"

"I am seriously in love with you," said Jasper.

She scoffed and turned away from him, but he was almost sure he saw a smile, and that was enough for him.

"You cannot just expect those…those feelings to be there, immediately," Opal said quietly.

"They are for me."

They were only a few inches from each other on the doorstep of Lord and Lady Romeril's, and Jasper found himself wishing they were a little closer. Close enough for his arm to brush against hers, for her to feel a tingle of anticipation, as he felt it.

Lord and Lady Romeril, after all. Prestigious names in Society, even Jasper knew of them. Had heard mutterings, good most of the time. Had seen her name in the gossip columns as a leader of fashion. How Opal had managed it, breaking into the Romerils' circle, he was not sure. They were far above them in station, but no one could surpass Opal for elegance and beauty.

Perhaps Lady Romeril wished to gather other elegant, fashionable women around her.

Or perhaps, whispered a vicious voice in the back of his head, *it was not Lady Romeril, but Lord Romeril who wished to know Opal a little better.*

Painful words stuck in Jasper's throat, both desperate to be spoken and swallowed. He coughed.

A comforting hand rested on his arm. Jasper looked to Opal, who was smiling.

"Look," she said quietly, the street behind them bustling with carriages taking people to their evening engagements. "We are…well. Still learning how to be a couple again."

Jasper smiled, his nerves surely showing on his face. "I know—but I want to be a part of your life again. And this is your life."

He jerked his head to the door.

Opal examined him for a moment, her blue eyes fixed upon him with a fierce look. Then she nodded. "Right. Well then."

Turning away, Opal reached out for the knocker.

Jasper tried not to stare, but it would be a difficult task all evening.

The door opened before them.

"Good evening! The Countess Marnmouth," Opal murmured, inclining a hand delicately to indicate the woman as they stepped into the hallway and into a drawing room that was far larger and more splendid than their own. "Oh, and I can see old Axwick is here, how unpleasant. I did not believe him back from the Continent. Ah, Lady Rose…"

Opal curtseyed low, and Jasper accompanied her in a bow to someone he did not recognize.

Blast. If only he had had the wherewithal to request that old Maltravers could also receive an invitation to dine. He would at least have had one friendly face in the crowd.

As it was…

"And the Braedons, of course," Opal said under her breath, smiling at a gentleman who waved from the other side of the room, causing Jasper's blood to pound in his ears. "And the

Derbyshires…"

More faces, more names Jasper was sure he would not remember. It was dazzling, almost making him dizzy, wandering from place to place with Opal's hand on his arm, guiding him as though a horse being put through its paces.

"You just sit here," Opal said firmly.

Jasper sat obediently as though a lapdog, finding himself in an armchair by the fire. And it was most pleasant, he had to admit. Even if he had the rather unpleasant sensation that Opal had deposited him here because he was…well. Getting in her way.

"Ah, Lady Romeril," Opal said smoothly, smiling as she curtseyed to the woman resplendent with pearls. "So lovely to be invited, I must say."

Lady Romeril said something Jasper did not quite catch, her eyes darting toward him, and Opal laughed merrily and waved a hand.

"Oh, him? Yes, I keep him around, far more interesting to have him than not, I am sure you find the same…"

Jasper grinned. The lapdog sensation was growing, but he could not find it within himself to care. Not with Opal speaking of him like that, with laughter and joy in her voice, and in public, too.

Sometimes, and this was one of those times, Jasper had to remind himself that he had indeed married her. She had chosen him when she could have had so many others.

"Ah, you must be Mr. de Petras."

Startled, Jasper rose to his feet and bowed to the gentleman who had addressed him. Opal had probably told him the man's name, but for the life of him, Jasper could not recall it.

He compromised by smiling tightly. "Yes, I am. I mean, I think I…yes. I am."

After being legally declared dead, Jasper thought darkly, he was not entirely sure how he should be addressed.

The gentleman nodded, his large cravat protruding past his chin. "I am surprised we have not met before. I am often at the de

Petras house—but then, who isn't?"

He laughed, but Jasper did not join him. His smile grew tighter, not reaching his eyes.

"Yes, always with Mrs. de Petras," continued the foolish gentleman, obviously not noticing the chill in their air. "Your wife is so charming, such wonderful company."

Opal was standing just a foot away, still in conversation with Lady Romeril, but Jasper knew she was listening to his own. There was surely no other reason why her cheeks should suddenly flush.

So. There had been more than one gentleman in contention. Not just Mr. King but a few other gentlemen quite willing to attempt to secure his wife's affections.

Well, in a way, he could hardly blame them. If he met Opal now, a widow with three children, he would certainly have tried for her.

"Wonderful company?" Jasper repeated, forcing himself to relax. "Yes, I suppose she is."

It was the merest of glances; if Jasper had blinked, he would probably have missed it. Opal glanced over at him, rolled her eyes, and within an instant, returned to her conversation with Lady Romeril.

"Yes, I have been…out of the country for a little while," said Jasper pleasantly. He should never have doubted her. "And I must say how pleasant it is to be back and enjoying her company."

"Yes, I can imagine," said the blissfully ignorant gentleman, putting his hands behind his back and puffing out his chest. "Yes, as I said to Mrs. de Petras only a few months ago…"

The man continued on, but Jasper was not listening. He was dull, this man whose name he could not remember, and there was someone far more interesting to be observing.

A loud cough made Jasper start, and when he blinked, the gentleman whose name he did not know came back into focus. He looked remarkably displeased.

"I am sorry," said Jasper honestly. *It was not the man's fault he was such a bore, after all.* "I was…momentarily distracted."

For some unknown reason, the man did not glower or frown but instead smiled. "Ah, say no more, my friend, say no more. No one would blame you, sir."

He glanced over at Opal himself, and Jasper grinned. Well, the man was not blind. Anyone could see how remarkable Opal was.

A gong went in the hall, and the guests of Lord and Lady Romeril looked around, their chatter quieting. It was time for dinner.

Without saying a word to his conversational companion, Jasper stepped across the room and offered his arm to Opal. The woman who, save a little paperwork, was his wife.

Opal looked at him warily, clearly conscious of everyone's eyes on them. But she had no choice, and Jasper had not intended to give her one. She took his arm.

Though he knew he should be thinking of decorum—waiting for Lord and Lady Romeril to go through first, then any dukes or earls who happened to be in attendance—Jasper could barely think, only feel.

The dining room was, if possible, even more splendid than the drawing room. Where did Opal find these people?

"I know traditionally husbands and wives do not sit together," came the almost jesting tones of Lady Romeril ahead of them, seated at the foot of the table, "but as you have been apart for so long, I thought you would appreciate it, Mrs. de Petras."

Jasper swallowed. Was it intended as an insult? He was not sure. So long absent from polite company, unaware of Lady Romeril's personality, he could not tell.

Glancing at Opal, he watched her incline her head graciously toward her hostess.

"Why, thank you, Lady Romeril," Opal said elegantly, allowing Jasper to help her into the chair indicated by their hostess, right beside her. "Thank you, Jasper."

Was there surprise in her face? Had she not expected him to

be attentive, to pull her chair out for her? His heart flickered with warmth. No. She did not expect it.

All the better for him, he supposed, when he went above and beyond. He was determined to show Opal just how much he loved her—how much she meant to him.

The rest of the company had entered now, taking their seats, and Jasper took his own between Lady Romeril and Opal. Then he swallowed. A plethora of forks lay before him, seeming to go on into eternity on his left-hand side. Surely no one in existence had ever needed so many.

He had been raised well, as a gentleman, educated at Oxford for a good many years, albeit a good many years ago—but never before had he seen such complexities as this.

"Ouch!" Jasper yelped, pain shuddering through his toes. Someone had trod on his foot!

"Be quiet!" hissed Opal.

Looking at her in abject confusion, Jasper saw she was smiling—and gently placing a finger on a particular fork.

Though his toes still hurt, Jasper relaxed. Opal was far wiser than he had given her credit for; she had spotted his confusion.

Picking it up as refined as possible, he murmured, "Thank you."

Was that a flush on Opal's cheeks? If so, it was a heady thought that he still had such an effect on her, even if it was not the sort he had hoped for.

"You are beautiful, you know."

"Oh hush," she said with a good-natured smile. "People can hear you. And that's the sixth time today."

"I do not care. I am fortunate to be by your side."

Opal's smile softened, and Jasper felt a rush of joy through his body as she said, "Well, I am actually rather pleased to have you by my side."

Their eyes met: a moment, a mere instant, a frisson between them, a look and a smile that meant nothing and yet meant everything. Jasper's whole body seemed to be shocked as though by lightning.

And then it was over. Opal looked at her food, taking a mouthful with the same fork she had just shown Jasper, and struck up a conversation with the gentleman on her other side.

Jasper had to swallow a few times before he got his breath back. Slow though it may be, they were meandering down the path toward discovering each other again. Hopefully, it wouldn't be too soon before his loving comments were loving kisses, then something more…

He froze. *Oh, no.*

"—really rather naughty of you," Lady Romeril said loudly—loudly enough for the whole table to halt their conversations and look at them. "Hiding your husband from us, Mrs. de Petras. Even going so far as to have him declared dead, you tease! Dangling your hook in the water to see if you could catch a bigger fish?"

Jasper could hardly believe he had heard such words. What rudeness! It was astounding anyone believed it acceptable to say such things at all—and in public, and so loudly!

No, he could not countenance it. Drawing himself up and opening his mouth, Jasper prepared himself to defend Opal and her honor.

As it turned out, he need not have worried.

"My dear Lady Romeril," Opal said sweetly with a sicky smile, "I have no idea what you are talking about. I do not believe anyone would believe I had purposefully been a part of such an error, and I can assure you if anyone, including yourself, had had the *manners* to ask, I would have told you the full and rather interesting tale. As it is, you can be sure your own nets still have as many fish as possible in the ocean for you to capture, though I do not believe your husband, Lord Romeril, is much interested in fishing?"

With a rather triumphant, yet genteel look, Opal took a sip of her wine and looked steadily at Lady Romeril.

Jasper almost applauded. He could never have responded to

such rudeness with such delicacy and strength.

Other conversations started to murmur around them, and Jasper leaned toward Opal. "I thought we were going to keep our heads down and ingratiate ourselves into Society?"

A wicked smile crept across Opal's face as she whispered back, "Is that not what I just did? Come, Jasper, you must learn the ways of polite—or rather impolite—Society. Lady Romeril is not loved, she is feared. I think we just made friends of everyone at this table."

Jasper shook his head with a wry smile. Opal de Petras did not need him to protect her, and this had been a sharp reminder of that fact.

Jasper could only hope, as he picked up his fork again and started eating, that he never got on her bad side again.

CHAPTER NINE

O PAL BREATHED IN the evening air. She blinked into the darkness, growing accustomed to the dimness after the bright candlelight of Lady Romeril's hallway.

"Well," she said softly. "That went reasonably well."

A tad of an understatement. Opal had desired a successful dinner, one that would introduce Jasper to her new London circle without any difficulty. A little light conversation, perhaps a jest or two, smiles all round, a pleasant meal, and they could slip away at the end of the evening with their heads held high.

But once again, this was a social situation she was leaving with Jasper that had not gone at all according to plan. That was the trouble with having a swift and biting tongue.

"Hiding your husband from us, Mrs. de Petras. Even going so far as to have him declared dead, you tease! Dangling your hook in the water to see if you could catch a bigger fish?"

Lady Romeril was the same as ever, and Opal should have known the more elegant woman would have attempted something to unsettle her.

Dangling your hook in the water, indeed…

Opal sighed heavily. She had been sorely provoked it was true, and she was proud of standing up for herself. Besides, there were advantages to such an outburst.

Smiling, Opal's fingers tightened around her reticule,

weighed down with numerous cards which had been slipped into her palm discreetly as the evening went on. It appeared she had been right when she had told Jasper they had won the admiration of everyone there.

Lady Romeril may never invite her back, it was true, but there would be plenty of other dining rooms now opened to the de Petras name.

Opal lifted her head to the heavens and wished—not for the first time—that London did not have so many fires and candles in the evenings. The smokey orange haze made it impossible, especially on cloudy nights like this, to see the stars.

They were there, somewhere. In Rome, one had only to travel a few miles from the city to see the splendor of—

"I thought the carriage would be here."

Opal lowered her head and smiled at Jasper, who was looking along the street. "I sent it home."

Jasper turned to her, a puzzled expression on his face. "Home?"

She nodded. "Well, no reason to keep the driver up into the small hours—we had no idea when Lady Romeril would release...I mean, when the dinner party would be over."

A smile danced across her lips, and Opal knew she was acting far more mischievously than she had any right to. She was a wife, a mother of three children. A mother should not be flirting in the street with the man who had been her husband.

Yet, something had shifted within Opal. Perhaps it was having Jasper by her side at dinner. She saw the envious looks shot her way by ladies up and down the table—and not merely those who were eligible and hoping for a handsome proposal.

No, even a few of the married ladies seemed astonished that such a man had been her husband, and Opal had to admit if only to herself, he was handsome. Charming.

It did not absolve him of all crimes, true, but the revelation of the letters... Opal had to admit that there was some reason as to why Jasper had suddenly disappeared from their lives.

Even if she did not like it.

"I thought…well. We could walk back," Opal confessed.

Why was her heart pattering so painfully? Agony after agony, it could never settle whenever her eyes locked with Jasper's.

There was something remarkable in his expression. A knowing smile, yet at the same time, uncertain. A way of holding himself that made her shiver. He was so…so masculine. So certain of himself in a way she never had been.

Jasper stepped toward her, now only inches away, yet he made no effort to reach out and touch her. Opal found herself ever so slightly leaning forward.

For the warmth, she told herself firmly. That was all. For the warmth. It was a cold night indeed, and she could not be blamed for wanting to lean a little closer to the man who, after all, she had married.

What did she want from him? Lord Romeril's wine had been plentiful, yet she had been careful to only take a few cups of it, else who knew what she might do or say in the heady company of Jasper de Petras?

"Walk back, you say?" His gaze flickered from her mouth to her eyes. "Interesting."

Opal's breath caught in her throat. It was as though they had been transported back in time, as though they were courting again. As though Jasper had just requested permission to walk her home in the lemon-heavy breeze of Rome.

As though they should really not be here together at all.

Something forbidden, deliciously dangerous, swept through Opal's heart, even though she knew it to be false.

Why was she no longer aware of what to do with her hands? How did hands hang at one's side—or was it better to bring them up, clasp them before her?

She was not a chit of one and twenty—she was a mother of three!

"Well, I think it's a wonderful idea."

Opal blinked. So lost in her thoughts, she had almost forgotten it was her turn to say something.

"Now why did I not think of that?" Jasper said brightly, glancing around the deserted pavement. "A walk home, in the dark. Brisk. I like it."

"You did not think of it because I am the one with all the good ideas," Opal found herself saying with a chuckle.

She had intended it as a jest, a continuation of the strange but rather tantalizing teasing they were engaging with. She had not expected Jasper's face to fall, as though he had been critiqued in a manner most unwelcome.

"I...I know," Jasper said quietly. "I have not forgotten anything, not a single thing. You think I would still be here, attempting to win your heart once again, if I did not remember how wonderful it was being your husband?"

Heat crept up Opal's décolletage, tightening her chest and making it far more difficult to breathe. She had not forgotten anything either. The way he made her feel and not just the sensual delights they had shared, though goodness knew she missed them.

She craved him as she had craved no other, and Opal knew it was the closeness of matrimony, of true affection, that was calling out to her.

The question was, would her heart answer?

The streets were not empty, though they were dark. A few people walked in groups. Further down a turning, they did not take, Opal was sure she could hear someone calling out their wares, ales and pies. Laughter poured out of a house to their left.

A gentle laugh. Opal turned her head swiftly and saw Jasper chuckle to himself, and a defensive surge rocketed through her chest.

"What?" she said.

Jasper shook his head, as though that explained things.

"What?" Opal repeated.

"I was just thinking how this reminds me of when we were courting," Jasper said. "Walking along the streets in Italy, knowing I couldn't touch you, wanting to…"

His voice trailed away delicately, though it left Opal in no confusion as to what else he was thinking.

Tingles of anticipated pleasure blossomed across her body. How could she deny it, deny herself? She and Jasper…so in sync, so perfectly aligned, thinking the same thing.

As they turned a corner, she was visited suddenly by a vision—or more a memory, of the very first time they had made love.

Their wedding night. Repressed urges and unbidden desires, heat and lust, and touching, kisses where kisses had certainly not been before…

The intensity of the memory that burst into Opal's mind was extraordinary as though she was returned to that moment, and she indulged in it, desperate to remember some of the happiest moments they had shared. The way he was so gentle, stroking her, the way he kissed her, held her—

Her delightful thoughts were rudely interrupted by a jerk on her arm—Jasper's hand had leapt forward to clutch her own.

"Jasper!" Opal said, almost in anger, astonished at the way he had so roughly held her.

She blinked. It appeared they had reached the edge of the pavement, though she had not noticed it. In an instant, a carriage rushed past them at a tremendous speed.

If it had not been for Jasper's foresight, his instincts to stop her, ignore her cry…

Jasper was breathing heavily. "Are you quite alright?"

Opal smiled, her own breath a little short. She had no wish to see her brains scattered across the road, and if he had not grabbed her hand…

Then something a little amusing struck her, and she could not help but smile. "You did not say anything."

"I beg your pardon?"

"You did not say anything," Opal repeated, then added, "You did not say 'be careful.' You remembered how much I disliked it."

Jasper returned the smile. "I...I meant what I said, you know."

Opal frowned slightly as they crossed the street a little more carefully this time. "That we were supposed to ingratiate ourselves into Society?"

Jasper shook his head with a laugh as they reached the other side of the road and continued along the pavement. "No, not that. That I only left because I truly believed harm would come to you. The idea anyone could threaten you, that I could suffer to live in a world without you..."

Opal heard the pain in his voice, watched a shadow darken his face, and waited as Jasper became incapable of speech.

There was love there. Not just love, but devotion. Was that not all she had ever wanted from him?

No, she needed to guard herself. Guard against the temptation to slip back into old habits, old ways. They were not her ways any longer.

"I suppose you could not have sent me a letter, let me know that you were safe? Merely knowing you were alive..."

Jasper glanced at her. "I thought about it. Agonized over it. It never seemed safe. Sometimes I do not realize how hard it was for you."

"No one can possibly know."

They continued on in silence for a few minutes—minutes in which Opal could berate herself for being too direct, not direct enough, too open, not open enough.

Words spoken in spite echoed around her mind.

"*...dangling your hook...*"

Opal sighed. "Thank you. For trying to defend me."

A frown tinged Jasper's forehead. "The carriage wouldn't have mounted the pavement to get to you, at least I do not believe it would."

"Not that," said Opal with a laugh. "At the dinner. Lady Romeril."

"Oh, you did not need my help," said Jasper ruefully. "You

were magnificent, as I should have expected. I should never have doubted you."

It would have been easy to preen, easy to accept his kind words without comment. But Opal knew that while he chased her, she had to start her own pursuit as well. She could not merely expect Jasper to prostrate himself at her feet without giving a little in return.

A very little.

"It is easier to be bold with you by my side. There have been other times…times when I did not have you. It was difficult to be so vulnerable. So alone."

"I know. I am sorry, Opal, you must believe me."

"It is hard," she said as lightly as possible, "to regain one's reputation."

"You seem to have done an excellent job at it," Jasper said fairly. "An invitation to Lady Romeril's table, and that was after my foolish actions at Almack's."

Opal glanced at him. Genuine regret sparked in his eyes, but as a few people passed them on the street, Opal found herself distracted.

She had never given much consequence to the strangers that passed her. This was London, after all. One passed strangers, hundreds of them, every day.

But now she had a far greater concern, and suspicions dulled the happiness which had been growing in her heart. What if the person who wrote those threatening letters was here, in London? Watching them? What if they had seen Jasper return to her?

"I know, it was a risk returning."

Opal started. There, he did it again, giving that strange sensation Jasper was listening to her most innermost thoughts.

"Yes, the letter writer could still intend harm," said Jasper with a heavy sigh. "But I couldn't live without you, Opal. Seven years was enough. If they were going to do something, surely they would have done it by now?"

They were almost home now, and it would be easy to push

aside the conversation, ignore it, and pretend it was not a problem.

But Opal could not. She was no fool, and neither was Jasper. "They did not wish to harm me—at least, not physically."

The instant the words had left her mouth, she regretted them.

Jasper stopped dead. "What do you mean by that?"

It would not do for Jasper to see just how afraid she was. She had to redirect him, misdirect him away from the truth. Or at least, her suspicions. She could not yet be sure if she was right.

"The letter writer—whoever they were—wanted me to suffer, can't you see? You were sent away from me, my…my husband. The one person I relied on. They caused me to suffer greatly without laying a finger on me."

Jasper nodded. "I did not even think of that. Someone really dislikes you, Opal—and you have no idea who it is?"

Opal hesitated. *Until she was sure…* "You know, I am getting rather accustomed to having you around."

"Good," said Jasper, taking a step toward her with a well-known look in his eyes, "for I intend to be for a long time."

Opal swallowed. Desire for and fear against what was about to happen warred in her heart, and she could not help but murmur, "Please—please don't hurt me again, Jasper. If y-you are just going to disappear again—"

"I promise I never will," he said in a low voice, then his lips were on hers, his mouth demanding her pleasure, his tongue teasing for entrance, and Opal let him.

Of course she did. After such an evening, such conversation, the sense of courting and desire in the air, how could she not?

Because he was her Jasper. The man she had married. Losing herself to the kiss, Opal's entire body awoke with pleasure as his lips ravaged hers, giving and demanding sensual pleasure, and before she knew it, she was pressed up against a wall, her fingers tightly woven into his hair, and she would never let him go, never.

It mattered not that they were standing on the street, his body covering hers as only a possessive husband could. Opal wanted him. She needed him. Whether she looked like a harlot or not, she needed a kiss from Jasper.

CHAPTER TEN

May 5, 1794

O PAL HAD NO thought that the following days would be any different. After all, she and Jasper had managed to find equilibrium with their daily routines—meals together, time with the children, wonderful conversations in the evening, and peacefully retiring at night—separately, of course.

He asked for no more, and she saw no reason to give it. It was, after all, a growing understanding of each other, and though at times she wondered just what would happen if she invited him into her bedchamber…

Opal swallowed as she descended the stairs. She could not wait forever. Mr. Cleland had been clear in his last letter; undoing Jasper de Petras' death certificate would be complex—and expensive—but not impossible.

Within days, he would exist again. Legally, that was.

And she would be faced with a decision.

Nothing looked altered when she reached the hall, and it was mere chance Opal decided to enter the drawing room before the breakfast room. She could hear the clatter of cutlery against crockery, the children breaking their fast with their governess, but Opal had been almost certain she had left the matching pair of her kid leather gloves in the drawing room, and it would be most irritating to be without it when she went visiting that morning.

Only when she opened the door did Opal's mouth fall open.

It was her drawing room...yet not her drawing room.

All the paintings which had adorned the walls were gone. The furniture had been moved around, some entirely removed, and in its place...

"My goodness," Opal breathed.

She had never believed it possible. Why, when she had first come to England, no matter how many experts she conferred with, they said it simply wasn't possible to find the same elegant style of furnishings she had grown up with in Rome.

But no longer. Her drawing room had been transformed, seemingly overnight, into an approximation of her Roman home. The place she had grown up in.

Landscape paintings of the Colosseum and St. Peters now adorned the walls, elegant light streaming down as only the classical artists knew how. There was a marble bust of what appeared to be a Roman emperor on the windowsill, and a harp in one corner that looked almost precisely the same as the one she had learned on as a child.

A bottle of what appeared to be amaretto sat happily beside two glasses on a console table—where an oak one had stood, and now an olive wood now stood.

Along the mantelpiece was a garland of olive branches decorated with lemons, their heady scent filling the air.

Opal raised a hand to her chest. It was not possible. She was dreaming; a strange dream, to be sure, but still. She could not believe her eyes.

"Do...do you like it?"

Opal looked to her left, where Jasper had sheepishly stepped through from the parlor. "It...you did this?"

He shrugged, though a smile spread across his face. "I know how much you missed parts of your home, and I thought...well. It would not be difficult to change."

"Not be difficult..." Opal breathed.

Not be difficult? When she had spent over ten years in this country, never able to find half the things he had managed?

"You would be surprised how easy it is to purchase this in Italy and ship them over," said Jasper with a dry laugh, "when one owns a ship or three."

Opal could not help but smile. Well, that at least explained how he had managed to find so many delightful and beautiful objects.

She stepped across the room, her fingers reaching out, unconsciously, to touch the marble. The elegance of the stone, the craft it had taken to create something so beautiful, so smooth, so perfect.

It was astonishing. He was astonishing. Jasper. Though he may shrug it all off as merely something he had achieved through his shipyard—which had of course helped—he had still gone to great effort to find such beautiful things, keep it secret from her, and move it all in overnight…

"I did not get rid of any of the other things, of course," Jasper said hastily, stepping toward her and then faltering. "I just thought…well. A piece of Italy for you."

Joy rose in Opal's heart as she took in more around the room. The books on the bookshelf were in Italian. A bowl of biscotti could be spied by an armchair.

It was all so lovely, so personal to her.

Affection blossomed as she looked around. He had done this for her, his love for her creating such a wonderful room—a place she could luxuriate in the things she loved and had had to leave behind.

"I…I suppose you think this will make me fall in love with you again," Opal said with a nervous laugh, hardly able to look at him.

After all, was it not working?

"I suppose I did not think it would hurt," Jasper said, and Opal had no choice but to look at him, her eyes drawn to him. "I considered attempting to recreate the night we first met—"

"Well, there are plenty of lemons," said Opal, pointing to the mantelpiece. "You know, they never smell as good when they have spent weeks on a ship."

He was only a few feet from her now. A shiver rushed through Opal's body. Having him so close, so tantalizingly close…

"You know you cannot merely recreate the same thing over and over again," she said, almost surprised to hear how breathless her voice was, "and expect me to just fall in love with you."

"I know that," Jasper said softly.

Opal swallowed. He knew that, but did she? How could she explain these feelings for him, other than love?

She knew it was love, knew it could be nothing else…but after such a long time, was love enough?

Jasper reached out a hand and Opal gazed into his eyes as his fingers brushed her cheek. "Opal—"

"Because I did not know you then," Opal found herself saying, hardly knowing where this foolish talk was coming but knowing she could not have her heart broken again. "I was young, foolish—"

"I know that," repeated Jasper, his hand now cupping her cheek. "Which is why, as I said, I did not attempt to recreate where we met. I chose some of your favorite things, and if you look around, you'll spot that not all of them are from Rome."

Opal turned her head, losing contact with Jasper's hand but desperately searching for what he could be referring to.

It took her a moment, but as her eyes took in the bouquet of flowers, her heart softened, her whole soul sinking into happy memories.

"The Lake District," she breathed.

"Just after you had Coral, do you remember?"

Did she remember? Opal could barely breathe, she was so overcome with emotions: joy, fear, memories of exhaustion, and yet perfect days. Days spent in sunlight and rain, the smell of the earth as the storm cleared and the sun blossomed once more. The gurgles of a baby, the sleepless nights spent with those you loved.

"I...I did not think you remembered," Opal breathed.

"Not remember?" Jasper chuckled, lowering his hand to his side. "You think I would not remember that?"

"It was so long ago," said Opal.

So long ago, and yet such a part of her that she knew she would never escape it. She had been in half a mind, when Jasper had disappeared, to retreat to the lakes. To where they had been so happy.

"I had been...well, exhausted," she said with a dry laugh, sinking down onto the sofa behind her, her legs suddenly no longer able to carry her. "Having a child was so much more than I had expected—"

"You had been wearing yourself to the ground."

"I did not know how to ask for help then."

Jasper took her hand in his; his fingers warm, firm. "You are not exactly excelling at it now."

They laughed together, Opal's heart fluttering. Yes, he was right. Who had she turned to after misplacing Jasper? Who had she relied on? No one. She had done it all alone.

"I thought you were mad, suggesting a holiday just a few months after Coral had been borne," she admitted.

Jasper raised an eyebrow. "You think you are just telling me that now? I know you, Opal. You could not keep that a secret, I promise you. Besides, I had been to the Lake District before. So peaceful, so calm...and that was what you needed. Peace."

He cared for her so much, far more than she had remembered. But she was remembering now. It was all coming back to her.

"That is why I thought...the flowers."

Opal looked up and glanced at the vase. "Wild angelica."

"Wild angelica," said Jasper with a smile. "It grew absolutely everywhere in the lakes, do you remember? And roseroot, they called it a weed and I just thought it was beautiful. You'd be surprised how difficult it is to find here in London."

She smiled, the buds reminding her of those halcyon days. Weeks they had spent there, away from the world, away from their lives, finally able to enjoy the child they had brought into the world. In a way, she had not wanted to go back. Had not wanted to face reality again.

"I can remember returning from a shoot with the local squire," said Jasper quietly, a hint of amusement in his voice, "though why I had been invited, I did not know—anyway, you were outside the cottage, sitting by the lake with Coral, humming a tune to yourself…it was as though the rest of the world had disappeared."

Jasper's fingers squeezed hers.

"I…everything felt perfect," Opal breathed.

"I thought I loved you the moment I first saw you," said Jasper gently, and Opal's gaze left the flowers and fixed on him, "and I did. I thought I loved you when we married, and I did. But nothing prepared me for seeing you as the mother to our children. Nothing prepared me for seeing you tired, ready to ask for help, help from me. When I knew you loved me as I loved you."

The devotion in his words, the longing in his voice, the desire rising up in her, the comfort, having her hands in his…it was too much.

"I have missed you," Opal breathed.

Jasper smiled. "I know."

"It's just—I do not know how to get back to that, to where we were all those years ago!"

"We cannot think like that," said Jasper softly. "We have to look forward—to what we can share in the future. Our future."

And she knew he was right, that all behind them could inform them, perhaps, but she could not try to live in the past. She could not live without him.

Leaning forward, Opal shyly touched her lips to Jasper's—then leaned further into his embrace as the shock of such pleasure rocked her body. Yes, this was where she belonged, in his arms, his lips on hers, sharing the exquisite pleasure she knew he could give her.

Jasper appeared surprised at first by her sudden show of affection, but he certainly did not hold himself back. One hand in her hair, the other at her waist, Jasper pulled her onto him as he leaned back on the sofa.

Opal gasped in his mouth, the kiss deepening as the wonderful sensation of her breasts pressed up against his chest caused shivers of sensual ecstasy to roll through her.

Oh, this was what she wanted, what she had missed, the connection that only a husband could offer.

"Opal," Jasper moaned, his hand moving to her buttocks, cradling her against him.

"Jasper," Opal breathed, suddenly conscious of a hardness pressing into her hip, almost flattered by the instantaneous response she had fired in him.

A sudden noise forced the two apart.

"What was that?" Opal said, sitting upright hurriedly and tucking a few strands of hair that had escaped her pins behind her ears.

Jasper groaned, still lying back on the sofa. "My cunning plan has gone awry."

Opal frowned. "I beg your pardon?"

"I had intended for the children to be out of the house far longer than that," he confessed with a sheepish grin.

It was impossible not to laugh as the door to the hallway opened, and a flurry of children and a dog rushed into the room.

"Mama, Admiral jumped in a puddle and got all dirty and—"

"Miss Matilda said we had to come home and wash him because—"

"Mother, look!"

"Don't let the dog onto the sofa," Opal said hurriedly, watching wet muddy dog prints spread across the room faster than she had believed possible. "Micah, no!"

Jasper collapsed into giggles as their son lifted up Admiral, who was coated in mud from head to toe onto the sofa, leaving an immediate damp patch.

"But Admiral's tired," protested Micah with wide eyes. "He needs a rest!"

Opal caught Jasper's eye and could not prevent herself from laughing as Emerald squeezed between them, chattering about just how large the puddle was that Admiral had jumped in. "So much for a peaceful courtship."

Jasper grinned. "You wouldn't have it any other way."

And Opal could not help but admit, even though it was only to herself, as Coral tried to carry Admiral out of the room to the kitchens, getting mud all over her gown, that she would not.

CHAPTER ELEVEN

May 8, 1794

JASPER GRINNED AS the children rumbled into the dining room like cattle marching across a field determined to find delicious food. Straw. Sometimes his metaphors got a little away from him, but there was certainly something vaguely animalistic in the way his children devoured their luncheon.

"About time, too!" he said easily, pulling out a chair for Emerald, who clambered up by herself. "I was about to send a rescue party to the nursery!"

Emerald giggled and gazed adoringly at her father, and Jasper felt a little more of his heart break.

Micah scowled as he sat silently at the other end of the table beside his mother, who had come in behind them.

Coral looked rather unimpressed, too, but for a different reason. "Do you not think I am a bit big to have it called a nursery, Mama?"

Oh, his Coral. Jasper beamed, unable to help himself. There had not been a single day that passed without Coral making it clear just how anxious she was about something, and her preoccupation with no longer being a little one was starting to show him just how much time he had missed.

Why, when he had last been with the family in Bath, she had

been…tiny.

And here she was, the ripe old age of twelve. It made his stomach twist a little, but Jasper pushed it away. He was getting better at pushing the regret away, though he did not know what that said about him.

Should he be pleased he was no longer feeling so darkly regretful—or was that concerning? Should he instead be feeling worse that it was so easy to brush aside?

Opal caught his eye from the other end of the table, raising a brow so clearly that Jasper knew precisely what she was thinking. Their children were getting on in years, and the term "nursery" evidently rankled their eldest. Time moved on, even if they did not wish it to. Even if Jasper wanted his children to stay little for just a few more years.

"I suppose so, Coral," Jasper said genially, "but you will always be my little one, no matter how big you grow."

His heart contracted as he watched Coral frown slightly, considering his words, then nod as though mollified by his approach.

No matter how big she grew. Jasper knew one day, Coral would be old enough to be attending balls of her own, dancing with someone other than her father, laughing at card tables—even finding a beau.

Beside him, Emerald picked up a slice of ham from her plate with her fingers.

"Fork, Em," called Opal down the table.

The child frowned at her mother, then obediently picked up a fork. Jasper watched her work it carefully; it seemed far too large for her tiny fingers.

"This is why the children usually have luncheon with the governess," Opal said quietly as she picked up her own fork and gave Micah a glare for good measure as he sullenly picked up his own.

But Jasper did not care. Manners. What care he for table manners? It was the time with his children he wanted desperately.

Ever since those kisses…those perfect kisses, Opal upon him on the sofa, desperation and desire overcoming him and, he rather thought, her, too. That primal need they shared to be close, to be together.

Whether or not the kiss had led to a physical release, Jasper could not help but feel that it had healed some of the wound between them.

"Here, let me help you, Em," Jasper said quietly.

Emerald obediently handed over her fork. Jasper used his knife and her fork to cut up her meat into more easily consumable bites and did the same with her vegetables for good measure.

He could feel Opal's eyes on him, but Jasper managed to prevent himself from looking up. He was not doing this for her. He was Emerald's father, and there was quite a bit of fathering he had to do.

"There you go, little one. That should be easier on your fork," he said in a low voice, handing the fork back to Emerald.

She beamed. "Thank you, Papa."

Looking up, he saw his rather sullen son had not touched his food. "Eat up, Micah."

"I'm not hungry."

Jasper's gaze moved to Opal instinctively. He had learned, painfully, that there were things about his children he simply did not yet know, and he was loathe to attempt to punish the boy for something that may be something more than he realized.

Was this mere fussiness, something that had to be encouraged out of the boy…or was this something deeper that he did not know?

Very delicately, so delicately Jasper was not sure whether he had seen it, Opal winked.

"Good," she said breezily, cutting into her meat with gusto, "for we had not intended to give you so much food anyway."

Micah looked at his plate, which had been filled by a maid.

"Come on, boy, put some back," Opal said cheerfully. "You can't possibly want all that meat—or the dripping. Why not give it to Coral?"

Micah glared furiously yet silently at his mother, picked up his knife and fork, and instead of returning the meat to the platter in the center of the table, started to eat.

Jasper stifled a very impolitic laugh. It would not do for his son to realize just how easily his mother had manipulated him, but it was rather amusing. Each and every day, Opal amazed him with the way that she was able to—lovingly—correct their children.

"Coral," he said aloud, more to distract himself than anything else. "Do you have everything you need? You do not have much."

One potato, one carrot, one slice of ham, and a little dripping. It would not have been much for Emerald, really, and from the stains on her plate, Jasper guessed Coral had in fact placed some of her food back onto the platters.

Coral took a prim bite of her food, obviously conscious to distinguish herself from her rowdy younger siblings. "I do not want to eat too much, there may not be enough for everyone else."

Jasper blinked. Everyone else? This was a family luncheon. They were not expecting anyone else—were they?

No, they could not possibly be. Meredith had only laid the table for five, and surely Opal would have said something if there needed to be an additional place setting laid.

"Or for later," said Coral. "One never knows how far a meal must stretch."

Jasper was entirely at a loss. Once again, he looked to Opal, who this time shook her head rather seriously.

"Coral, I have told you, we are not poor. We never have been, and with your father back...You can eat as much as you would like."

Poor? Jasper almost snorted. Nothing like if the ledgers were anything to go by. No, he would rather describe them as rich than poor.

Coral nodded, yet she took no more food. Instead, her gaze dropped to her food as though she wished to savor the sight of it just as much as the taste.

Jasper looked at his own plate, and his stomach nudged him. Picking up his fork, he took a bite of the delicious meal.

Coral's gaze had slipped from left to right between her parents a few times before she said, "You seem happier, Mama. And you, Papa."

Jasper cleared his throat as heat billowed up his neck, thankfully hidden by his cravat. *Blast.* Coral once again proved that her age was no measure of how perceptive she was. How on earth had she noticed that?

"Are you well, Papa?" asked Emerald anxiously, her forehead creased in a frown.

"Quite well, thank you," he said to Emerald, then smiled at Coral, who was evidently still waiting for an answer. "Things were perhaps a little strange while I was away, but now I am back, and that makes your mother and me very happy."

Perhaps he should not have spoken on Opal's behalf. For a split second, Jasper caught Opal's eye and saw a sardonic smile there the children would certainly have not understood.

Well. Perhaps Coral.

"Now we can be a family together again," said Jasper with a smile. "You are pleased to have me back, aren't you, Coral?"

It was a mistake. Jasper knew that the moment the words had come out of his mouth. Opal's knife and fork halted, her gaze still focused on her food but evidently astonished he had been so bold as to ask one of their children that.

Coral considered for a moment, a moment that seemed to stretch into eternity. Then she nodded and returned to her food. Words were apparently not necessary.

Jasper took a deep breath. "Have you been thinking about going to school, Micah?"

It was, after all, a reasonable question. The boy would soon be old enough for school, and there were plenty of sufficiently impressive ones to which they could apply.

But to Jasper's astonishment, it was not Micah but Coral who answered.

"School?" she said, alarm clearly painted on her face. "Will we be able to afford to send Micah to school?"

Opal laughed while Jasper stared at his eldest in confusion.

"Darling, of course we can," said Opal with a smile.

A flicker of worry rippled across Coral's face, and Jasper knew he had to say something to appease her concerns.

"Coral," he said quietly, "you are only twelve years of age. You are not meant to worry about that sort of thing—leave that for your mother and me."

"Of course, I worry!" said Coral, her voice tightening, and her cutlery abandoned on her plate. "How will we be able to afford years and years of Micah at—"

"You let us worry about that, Coral de Petras," said Opal firmly.

After a heavy huff, Micah slipped off his chair.

"Micah!" Jasper called after him.

Almost to get a little reassurance, Jasper glanced at Opal. She shrugged. It appeared the root cause of Micah's current sulk was just as unknown to her. Boys.

Emerald giggled, half her food gone and a good third of it down her front—though now Jasper looked a little more carefully, there was a snuffling noise by his feet. He lifted up the tablecloth. There Admiral sat, very happily, his nose in Emerald's lap, his chops covered in gravy.

Jasper looked at his youngest child, ready to reprimand her for feeding the dog at the table, but she spoke before he could.

"You are so naughty, Micah!"

"No, I'm not!" snapped Micah, coming back to the table.

It happened in an instant. Previous peace and calm disappeared as the two younger de Petrases bickered across the table, name-calling and teasing far beyond what Jasper could have imagined.

"Don't fight!" cried Coral over the top of them, but it seemed merely to increase the rivalry between Micah and Emerald.

Jasper looked bewildered at Opal, who was smiling and shaking her head. Apparently, this was a common predicament. Well, they did not have to sit here and wait for the children to wear themselves out. Besides, he was not sure his head could put up with much more of this clamor.

Rising without a word, Jasper pulled the bell over the fireplace. Within a moment, Meredith had appeared.

"My children appear to have far too much energy," Jasper said cheerfully to the maid as he sat back down, Micah and Emerald ceasing their shouting. "Please ask Miss...Miss Whatsherface—"

"You really must learn the governess's name, Jasper!"

"But I haven't finished luncheon!" Coral said bitterly. "And—"

"I will give Miss...Miss Whatever she calls herself—"

"Miss Matilda, Jasper!"

"Miss Matilda some shillings," said Jasper firmly. "She can purchase some sweet pastries on your visit to the park. Your immediate visit to the park."

Coral turned anxiously to her mother, who forestalled her concern immediately.

"A few shillings will not make us destitute, Coral, I promise," said Opal firmly. "Go!"

The three children filed out of the room, and Jasper leaned back on his chair and sighed. *Peace and quiet. Finally.* "I do not know how you have done it on your own."

For the second time during luncheon, Jasper wished he had not spoken. It was an insensitive thing to say, a cruel thing. Of course, she had struggled.

But Opal's smile was not bitter. "I can see you squirming, Jasper."

"I still think there are some things I shouldn't be saying to you. Things I should think, rather than say."

"Perhaps. But I want us to be back to the way things were

when we could be completely open with each other."

Jasper smiled as he took in the luscious view. She was about to play a dangerous game with him if she was not careful, though she did not yet know it.

"Truly, anything?"

Opal nodded, though a slight flush rose in her cheeks, as though she could guess what he was going to say. "Within the bounds of reason, of course."

Sighing heavily, Jasper shook his head in mock exasperation. "Now that's a shame."

"What do you mean?"

"Because what I want to say to you certainly isn't within the bounds of polite society." Jasper rose as he spoke, moving around the table. Here they were together, with the house practically empty. *It was the perfect time.*

Taking Opal's hand in his, his fingers tingling at the contact, Jasper looked deep into Opal's eyes. "You and I have some unfinished business."

"I...I don't know what you mean," Opal whispered, but her flush deepened, and Jasper felt the quicken of her pulse.

She knew precisely what he meant.

"I think you do."

Opal hesitated, her gaze seemingly unable to pull away from his, which was precisely what Jasper wanted to see. He wanted to see her desperate for him, wanting him, craving him.

"I..."

She was unable to continue as Jasper lifted her hand to his mouth and kissed it, lightly at first, then hard as though branding her with his own mark.

"You cannot tell me you have not thought of it. Of me. Of the two of us together."

Jasper spoke quietly, knowing that if he rushed this he would be swiftly shoved out of the room. But Opal did not look away. Her gaze lingered on his eyes for a moment, then dropped to his mouth.

Certain that now was the time to press home his advantage, Jasper allowed the longing he felt to seep into his voice. "It has been so long, Opal, and I know you have missed me. I want you. I want all of you. Don't you want me?"

CHAPTER TWELVE

THE HEAT RISING from her décolletage was not embarrassment, and so Opal did not look away from Jasper as he
examined her closely.

No, it was not embarrassment. It was desire.

How long had it been since she had tasted of it—really tasted?
Oh, the flirtations with Mr. Ransome and a few other gentlemen
had come close. She had seen the potential for desire there,
spotted that it could be possible. In time.

Opal shivered, despite herself, her hand still in Jasper's unre-
lenting grip.

"I want all of you. Don't you want me?"

Yes, she wanted him. Wanted him more than anything, more
than she thought possible. More than she could believe.

Opal did not move, and as the sensation moved through her
body, prickling uncomfortably, she knew what it was.

Fear.

The moment she permitted Jasper not only in her bedchamber but her heart, that would be it. She would be entirely
besotted once again. She would be vulnerable again.

"Opal," Jasper whispered, his eyes not leaving hers. "I will not
hurt you again."

Opal swallowed, almost cried out, desperate to hear him say
it again. She could not bear it; her heart would not survive such

pain again. And he knew that. Jasper knew her.

"You…you are certainly a man who knows what he wants," Opal said weakly, knowing she had to say something, hating the silence almost as much as her indecision.

A lopsided grin fell across Jasper's face. "I have always known, Opal. You think I would have sacrificed time in your bed if I had any other choice?"

Tempting as it was to merely laugh and then fall into his arms, Opal knew there was one more question that she had to ask. One more snippet of insight she had to ascertain before she could give her heart completely.

"Well, for all I know," Opal said tightly, "you have had plenty of other ladies in that bed of yours. While you were away."

There. It was spoken. Opal's stomach twisted painfully as she watched Jasper's face for any hint of an answer that may be betrayed in his features before his lips could open.

His grip on her hand tightened, but the other lifted to her cheek, cupping it, and was all softness.

"Opal," said Jasper seriously, smile gone and eyes fixed on hers, "I was never unfaithful to you. Never. I could not even imagine it, it-it—it would be unfathomable."

Opal looked deep into his eyes and wanted to see the truth in them. Was she fooling herself, her desperation to believe him clouding her judgment?

She loved him. She desired him. She was a woman, and she had needs—needs that had not been met for seven long years.

Opal swallowed. "You…you are sure about this?"

"More sure than anything," said Jasper softly. "I love you, and you are my wife. Should be my wife. I want you by my side."

A slow smile crept across Opal's face as she rose to her feet, not letting go of Jasper's hand. "I am already by your side."

"You know full well that that is not what I meant," said Jasper darkly, a little growl in his voice. "I want you in my bed, Opal. Our bed."

A shiver of anticipation rustled down Opal's spine. It did not feel entirely real; it was the middle of the day, for goodness' sake! They were no longer young things, newly married, unable to help themselves, unable to prevent themselves from falling into bed at any moment.

But her body did not know that. It was sparking alive already with the memories of what had come before, the hope of what was about to come now.

Perhaps the only way to find perfection at this moment was not to hold onto control with an iron grip but to…let go.

"I have missed you, Opal," Jasper breathed, his lips mere inches away. "Let me show you how much."

"Only if you catch me first."

Her instincts had finally won the day, and Opal laughed as she saw Jasper's startled face as she pulled her hand away and darted toward the door.

"You little—"

Opal squealed with delight, heart thumping wildly as she heard Jasper follow her into the hall, chasing after her, half-muttered oaths on his tongue—and then she was flying up the stairs …

As though they were about to experience each other for the first time.

"Jasper!" Opal yelled, unable to help herself as she reached the top step, but a hand grabbed her, pulling her back.

For a heart-stopping moment, she hung there, falling down the stairs, arms flailing but unable to save herself—until a pair of strong hands caught her and pulled her close.

Jasper's hands. She was in Jasper's arms, and Opal blinked at him, feeling his strength, feeling the certainty of his presence.

He was panting. So was she.

"Damn, woman," Jasper said in a jagged voice. "You are so beautiful."

Opal knew what was coming, knew she could avoid it if she wished, but she had no instinct to. She wanted Jasper to kiss her, take her mouth and possess it, the tingling across her lips deepening and spreading across her body as the kiss deepened.

This was where she belonged, in Jasper's arms as she gave herself up to the sensuality of it all.

Finally, and Opal could not have guessed how much time had passed, Jasper pulled away with a wry grin. "Is this when you finally permit me entrance to your bedchamber?"

"You know," said Opal, "no man has ever stepped in there before."

"I am glad to hear it," Jasper growled, lifting her up and carrying her the final few steps to the landing.

"I am hardly a newlywed, Jasper, put me down!" laughed Opal, her head spinning, unsure what was going to happen next. "We have three children!"

But was this not one of the reasons she had fallen in love with Jasper in the first place? His ability to do anything, beyond reason, beyond expectations. Life with him had never been dull. It never would be.

When Jasper reached her bedchamber, Opal turned the handle, and he stepped inside, carefully placing her on the bed before turning to close the door behind them. He turned the key with a satisfying click, and Opal shivered.

This was it, then.

"I know this is no true honeymoon," said Jasper quietly. "But I want this to feel special—as special for you as it is for me. I feel like after missing out on so much, I can finally be your husband again."

Opal knew precisely what he meant, though she could not have put it so eloquently. There was something more than parenting that made a husband—a closeness, a connection one shared with no other.

And that had been missing. Every minute that Jasper had been back in her life, their lives, she had felt it. Felt the dissonance created by this false distance between them.

But now, finally, Jasper had truly come home. This was the man she fell in love with, the man she married. The man she wanted back in her bed.

"Jasper," Opal whispered, reaching out to him.

He needed no further invitation. She was not sure how he managed it, but within an instant, Jasper was in her arms, his mouth on hers, and it was too much, too wonderful, too glorious. Hidden depths of herself were being opened up again, parts Opal had been certain would remain dormant for the rest of her life.

Every inch of her body shivered as pleasure started to pour through her, building, growing, teasingly warm, and yet not quite enough.

Jasper had already managed to wrench off his justacorp and waistcoat, and Opal raised her fingers to his shirt, pulling at the buttons hastily.

A smile crept across her face as she pulled the shirt up over his shoulders. There were the muscles she knew so well, the raw strength that had warmed her all those years ago.

"You have not changed a bit since we last..." Opal thought just how the years had changed her own body.

Since they had last made love, since Jasper had last seen her... Seven years, and the birth of a child.

Jasper kissed her cheek delicately, as though he knew precisely what she needed. "I know. 'Tis most unfair that I am the same, yet you are more beautiful."

Opal chuckled. "Flatterer."

"Of course," said Jasper, his attention now moving to her gown.

Slipping off the bed to give him better access, Opal tried not to think about the layers of silk and satin being removed from her body as he undressed her.

Jasper groaned as his fingers reached her corset, stiff bones and complex knots. "I had forgotten how difficult it was to get you out of these."

Opal laughed. "Oh, I wouldn't say that. Surely that's half the fun?"

A strange look shadowed Jasper's eyes, and Opal shivered.

There was something about the way he looked at her. As though he wished to devour her, as though making love to her would never be enough.

"You are absolutely right," said Jasper quietly. "Half the fun…"

His fingers left her corset and instead trailed across her décolletage. Opal quivered with the heady sensuality but did nothing, merely standing there, allowing herself to be touched. Oh, how she wanted to be touched.

"Jasper!" she gasped.

His fingers had suddenly dropped to the bottom of her corset, to her thighs. Stroking them delicately, Jasper watched her, as though wanting to see what he did to her.

Opal couldn't think; she could only feel.

Still silent, Jasper walked around her, and Opal moaned slightly as she heard him remove his boots and breeches. Oh, not being able to see him, knowing he was right behind her and—

"Jasper," she whispered.

It was not a plea, merely the suggestion of one, but it was enough to spur him into action. Opal gasped as she felt his warmth behind her, embracing her. Jasper kissed her shoulder delicately, making Opal whimper as his fingers started to undo the knots of her corset.

Slowly, slowly, with more kisses up her neck and the heady suggestion of his bare thighs against hers, the corset came undone. It was thrown aside, along with Opal's chemise and petticoats.

And that was it. She was naked.

Opal turned slowly and quivered with anticipation as she saw Jasper. He was precisely as she had remembered him—handsome, the man she had welcomed into her bed all those years ago.

"Jasper."

He pulled her into his arms at that murmur of invitation, and Opal groaned with happiness as the intensity of the moment overwhelmed her. Jasper's skin against hers, nothing between them, nothing holding them back from each other. It was all she wanted—and she was very certain of what she wanted next.

Overcome by desire, Opal pulled Jasper to the bed and into her arms. They would make love slowly, carefully, lovingly, later, many times.

But right now, passion ruled her, driving her forward, rushing through her body and it could not be denied.

"Enter me," Opal begged.

Jasper's eyes widened, his legs nestled between hers. "You—you are sure?"

Opal moved a hand to his manhood, and he groaned, his eyelashes fluttering as he gave himself up to the pleasure. "I need you, now."

Jasper did not need further invitation. They both moaned with pleasure as he entered her, slowly, inch by inch, and Opal knew she was about to be completed in a way she had lacked for seven long years.

"Damn, you are better than I remember," Jasper moaned in a jagged whisper, "and you were good then."

It was all Opal could do to focus on his words. There was no possibility of replying. Her mind was dazzled with growing sensations, the hardness of him within her, the desperate ache that needed to be quenched.

"Take me," Opal said, her fingers clinging to his shoulders, needing him deeper, needing movement, anything to fan the flames of the fire within her. "Please, Jasper, take me, take me now!"

Jasper moaned as he dipped his head to kiss her, passionately entangling his tongue with hers, before he broke off the kiss and looked deep into her eyes.

"You have no idea how much I have dreamt of you saying that."

Opal arched her back as Jasper pulled out almost all the way, then thrust back into her. Sparks of ecstasy shot through her, and she could not help but whisper his name, which only seemed to push him further.

Faster, and deeper, and Opal lifted her legs, her ankles in the air as she welcomed him in, her whole body shivering with a growing warmth, pleasure rushing through her in waves, building, building, the ache in her desperate for relief. She was close, so close, and she cried out to let him know.

"Oh, Jasper, yes, yes, there, more!"

And that was it. Opal fell apart as she cried out in ecstasy, and Jasper poured himself into her, unable, it seemed, to hold himself back as the cries of their lovemaking intermingled and eventually fell silent.

# CHAPTER THIRTEEN

May 9, 1794

JASPER BLINKED. THE bedchamber came back into view slowly. It had a strange pattern to it; light from the window was scattering shadows across a wallpaper he recognized.

He blinked again.

Memories poured in from the previous night. Memories of pleasure, of kisses, embraces, and knowing that he had finally, after all this time away, come home.

"Take me. Please, Jasper, take me, take me now!"

Opal. Jasper leaned heavily against the pillow, relief tinging his stomach—they had made love.

And it was not just once. There had been some particularly wonderful moments as the candlelight flickered, and they had taken their pleasure again and again.

They had spent all afternoon in bed together. The children had come back, Jasper had heard them, and Opal had taken a moment to instruct the governess and maid on what to do with them—but for the first time, perhaps in her children's life, she had put herself first.

A small miracle.

After lovemaking, whispered sweet nothings, and declarations of love and hope and adoration, he and Opal had curled up and talked. And sat in silence. Just hearing her heartbeat, knowing Opal was close, that she trusted him, that she still loved him, it completed him.

Those had been the most precious moments of all.

A weary smile crept across Jasper's face. *Finally.* After hesitation and fear, confusion, and moments when he had believed nothing could be repaired, everything was as it should be.

He had convinced Opal de Petras he loved her, that his entire life had been, still was, and always would be, committed to her. There was none more important than her. His Opal.

There was not a single thing he would have changed, and he had to hope Opal would be of a similar mind. *And speaking of Opal…where was she?*

Jasper sat up, suddenly conscious he was in the large bed alone. Why would she leave without him?

The door opened, and Opal strode in, fully dressed and hair adorned. Suddenly conscious he was entirely naked and aware that anyone could walk in behind Opal and see him, Jasper pulled the bedclothes protectively over his chest.

Opal laughed as she closed the door. "Do not worry, it has been a while since the children have come into my bed."

My bed. Not our bed. Jasper could not blame her, he supposed. There were years of learned behavior they would both have to unlearn, different for each of them.

"I was not expecting you to be up so early," Jasper confessed with a grin.

Opal raised an eyebrow as she moved to the window and pulled open the curtains to reveal blazing sunlight. "Early? 'Tis near eleven o'clock in the morning, Jasper. I came here to wake you before luncheon."

Jasper's mouth fell open. *Near eleven?* How was it possible that he had slept so long?

Opal's grin broadened. "I was the only parent for a while, remember. I was always the one to get up early, always the one that had to be available, ready at a moment's notice."

Jasper smiled weakly.

"To be honest with you, I am looking forward to the time when you can get up early and leave me in bed," teased Opal, leaning against the windowsill. "Now," she said firmly, "I am taking Coral to the modiste."

"The modiste," Jasper repeated vaguely. *Had Opal mentioned this before?* Was he supposed to know what this was all about?

Opal's knowing look suggested he should. "A new trio of gowns, Jasper, as we discussed—it does not matter. She is growing so fast, she needs new clothes, and I shall ask Madame Jacques to make them a little longer, perhaps with a tuck so they can be let out as she continues to grow."

"Don't let Coral hear you say that," Jasper teased. "She will worry we may not be able to afford gowns for her in the future."

"Lord, yes, I shall keep that to myself and speak very delicately in Madame Jacques's ear," said Opal with a sigh. "Miss Matilda is taking care of the other two upstairs."

Jasper nodded.

In an impetuous movement, Opal stepped over to the bed, leaned over, and kissed him. "I shall miss you, Jasper de Petras!"

Well, he could not help it, could he? With Opal so close once again, and the memories of their kisses lingering at the edges of his mind, Jasper did the only thing he could think of: placed his arms around her and pulled her into the bed with him.

"Jasper de Petras, let me go!"

"Never," he said happily. "You are my prisoner, and I will not let you leave without a kiss."

Opal squealed with laughter just as she had done when they had first married, pecked his cheek, and wriggled free. "Really! My appointment with Madame Jacques—"

"Yes, yes, fine," he said, plumping up the pillows so he could lean against them. "Next time, tell me. I'd like to come."

That was apparently not the correct thing to say. Shaking her head as she laughed, she said, "Jasper, you cannot think to come to the modiste! 'Tis for ladies, ladies only!"

Jasper shrugged. "Well, perhaps not the modiste itself—but I do not want to be left behind Opal, always hearing about things that are happening and not taking part. I want to be a part of their lives, Opal. And yours."

He had attempted to put heart into those words, though it afeared him slightly to say them. To be so open…it was not the English gentleman's way.

But she seemed to understand. At the very least, Opal smiled but stayed silent, closing the door quietly behind her as she left.

As Jasper was not actually needed anywhere, per se, he made use of his time in bed, basking in the glow of knowing that he and Opal had finally managed to put the past behind them.

Painful, it had been. Slightly torrid, it certainly was. But now they had the rest of their lives to better understand each other. To love each other.

When he did finally get up, Jasper let out a groan. He was not as young as he once was.

It took a moment to pull on breeches and his other clothes scattered around the floor, then he leaned out of the door into the corridor to check that no one would see him sneaking back to the guest bedchamber to retrieve a fresh shirt.

As Jasper slowly did the buttons up, he looked around the guest bedchamber in a different light.

He had not chosen this house. Opal had found it alone, though perhaps Coral might have given her opinion. He would have to ask. The wallpaper and carpets were certainly of Opal's choosing. Jasper would recognize that taste anywhere— flamboyant, yes, but elegant. A delicate mixture.

Something akin to regret, but not quite as bitter, rose in Jasper's heart. Their home in Bath had been elegant and refined, something they had built together. Every decision had been made as a pair, though it was Opal's money that had purchased it and her wealth that had furnished the place. His had been reinvested in the shipyard, a third ship to grow the company.

Yet she had never made him feel as though it was not his

home. Not like this place.

He should have returned earlier.

The thought flashed through his mind in an instant, painful but impossible to disagree with. It was easy now, with the beauty of hindsight, to think that the letter writer—whoever they were—was just nonsense. A jest gone wrong.

But during such a sense of fear, with the Terror going on in France and anyone who was not English being targeted…

Jasper's jaw tightened as he came to the last button. He had taken the threatening letters seriously, and who knew what might have happened if he had not. He could be a widower now, with no children. Staying had not seemed an option.

But now he had reunited with Opal…nothing had occurred.

No retribution. No return of the letters, which was half what Jasper had expected.

Perhaps there were additional clues he could fathom from the letters themselves. Yes, that would be an excellent use of his day today, while Opal and the children were engaged. He would never be able to rest, not entirely, until the mystery of the letters had been solved.

Striding across the guest bedchamber, now fully dressed save for his cravat, Jasper opened his trunk for both cravat and letters.

Only the former was there.

It took him a moment to recall, but only after he had tied his cravat did Jasper remember why. Of course, he had given the letters to Opal as evidence of why he had left.

So, they would be…downstairs?

A wide smile was on Jasper's face as he half walked, half ran down the stairs and across the hall to the drawing room. There was nothing to dim his mood today, not now he and Opal were once again on a happy footing.

The bureau was against the wall on one side by the grandfather clock, and when Jasper opened it, a flurry of paperwork fell out. Opal must have filled the thing to bursting. Most of them were bills or invoices, from what Jasper could see. They all had variations of 'PAID' stamped across them in red ink.

She truly was a marvel. Jasper could not comprehend how Opal had managed to mother three children, keep a household running, and maintain a small yet secure place in Society.

There—his eye caught the bundle of letters, and Jasper pulled them toward him. Only when they were in his hands did he realize they were not the letters that had threatened his wife with violence if they decided to remain together.

No, these were letters of quite a different kind. A flurry of words on the top of the pile caught Jasper's eye.

astonished to have met such a beautiful woman as

Jasper swallowed. That was a wooing sentence, but he could not recall…

He removed the top letter from the pile and glanced at the one underneath it.

enchanted from the very first moment I met you, and knew

Slowly, very slowly, Jasper lowered himself into an armchair. They were not the letters he had been looking for—but nor were they courting letters he had sent Opal from times gone by.

He had not sent her many. They had been wed too quickly for much correspondence.

Knowing he was doing something wrong but unable to help himself, Jasper untied the string around the pile of letters and started to flick through them.

never felt this way for any other lady, and I beg you
could not comprehend a world in which you did not
must ask you to consider my offer, I will not call it a proposal

Only after reading one in full did he realize what they were. Love letters. Love letters to Opal—from a gentleman he did not know.

Blood boiling, heart pounding, Jasper tried to keep calm, but it was impossible. That she would betray him like this—the things the man was saying, it was obscene!

Pain tore through his heart. Jasper raised a hand to his chest as though that could prevent the agony, but it did nothing. How had he managed to become so vulnerable? He had ignored all opportunities to be unfaithful, feeling his heart bound entirely to Opal. He had expected the same devotion, the same loyalty.

And who had sent her such…such suggestive letters? One of the gentlemen he had met here—the stupid one he had thrown out of the house? Mr. King? He should have called out the devil!

"—show her the paid invoice, she is much mistaken," came Opal's voice from the hall. "Madame Jacques knows I always pay my bills on time—it'll be here, in the bureau."

Jasper rose hastily but there was no point—he would never have had time to reach the bureau, let alone place the letters and all the bills back inside. He was still holding the letters, standing like a fool by the armchair when the door opened and Opal entered.

"You will never believe the nonsense Madame Jacques is trying to feed me," Opal said. "Arguing I did not pay for Emerald's last gown, as though…Jasper."

Her gaze flickered from the open bureau to the letters in his hand.

"What are you doing, snooping through my things?"

"We are—were—should be married," said Jasper coldly, taking a step forward. "They are *our* things."

"No, they are *my* things," Opal contradicted, stepping forward. "My bills, my invoices, my—"

"Letters?"

Jasper raised his hand holding the love letters and was careful to watch Opal closely. The flush, when it arrived at her cheeks, was dark.

Perhaps that was what hurt most of all. She could have pretended not to know them, that they were nothing to do with her. But guilt was painted across her face.

Tempting as it was to erupt, however, Jasper managed to hold his tongue. He loved Opal, knew it had been…strange between them. He owed her the chance to explain.

"Nothing…nothing actually happened," Opal said awkwardly. "I-I was lonely."

"So lonely that you—"

"I did not write to him!" Opal spoke quickly, pain in her eyes. "I never replied to a single one, Jasper, you must believe me. And how was I to stop such…such missives?"

"You still read them," he pointed out.

Opal hesitated for a moment, then held her head high as she met his gaze. "I did. As I said, I was lonely."

Jasper let out his breath in a long, slow heave. It was a relief to hear Opal had never compromised herself by responding to such letters. The idea that somewhere out there in the world were love letters from Opal to another gentleman…

They already had one scandal to overcome, his sudden reappearance. The last thing they needed was a second. The last thing this family needed was more gossip.

"So. He wrote to you."

Jasper had intended it as a statement rather than a question, but Opal looked abashed as she spoke. "It was a few years ago. I had accepted that you were never coming back, and I was lonely. I…I flirted. Once. In company, of course."

He needed to hear nothing more as the pangs in his heart started to subside.

"If I had known then…if I had known you were alive, that you were coming back, that you had not abandoned me—"

"You would not have read them?"

There was a rather knowing smile on Opal's face, one that Jasper could not help but like. "I would not have needed to. Surely you can understand that? I wanted…I needed reassurance. That I was beautiful. That I was worth desiring."

It was difficult to judge when hearing her speak so openly like that. Lord knew Jasper could not comprehend just how damaging his sudden disappearance had been.

"I am sorry."

Opal frowned. "You are sorry?"

"For reading them. Well, not all of them, some of them," said

Jasper with a heavy sigh. "I suppose this is part and parcel of our life now. There are…gaps. In our story together. Gaps taken up with other things."

"But not other people," said Opal. "I hope you can believe that."

And Jasper found to his surprise he could. She was his Opal. She would not lie; she had no need to. No real blame could be apportioned to a woman who believed herself a widow.

"I was actually looking for the threatening letters, to see if there were any clues I had missed about who had sent them."

Jasper could not help but notice Opal's entire body relax as the topic changed. "Ah. Well, here they are."

She stepped to the bureau to retrieve them, and in doing so, came very close to Jasper. He took his chance.

He kissed her lightly on the head and sighed. "I am sorry for reading them."

"I suppose I could say the same thing!" Opal said with a laugh as she placed the letters he had been searching for in his hands.

Jasper looked down at them. They contained far less pleasant words. "Have you had any other thoughts about who could have sent these violent letters?"

It was just the perception of an instant. If he had not been looking quite so closely, perhaps Jasper would have missed it. But he could not help but notice that Opal's jaw clenched, just for a fraction of a second, as she looked away.

"I…I have a complicated family history, back in Italy," said Opal quietly, stepping away. "But nothing that should have actually hurt us."

That was new. Complicated family history? Jasper had met Opal's mother, a good woman, now sadly gone—but nothing about her had appeared to be particularly complicated.

So, what did Opal mean? What did she not what to tell him? Why would she keep the potential perpetrator of such a scheme a secret when it had robbed them of seven years together?

"Well," Jasper said awkwardly, "then who? Who would want

to see us apart, separate, and alone?"

Again, Opal did not meet his gaze. "There may be…someone. A someone in my past."

Her past? "What do you mean?"

Jasper's heart fluttered painfully. Finally, they were starting to understand what could have led them to be so unhappy for so long—but just as Opal opened her mouth, the door opened and a hurricane entered.

"Coral's blaming me for spilling ink on the harpsichord, and it wasn't me, it was Coral. I haven't done anything wrong!"

"Micah de Petras, you liar! It was Micah, Mama, and I can prove it. I would never take ink near the harpsichord!"

Jasper blinked in the sudden rush of noise, and Opal smiled before turning to the children. "One at a time, please! Micah, you go first."

Jasper watched as Opal attempted to hear their stories over their impassioned sobs.

That was the trouble with children, one could not have a proper conversation! And that one, in particular, sounded important. Who on earth was in Opal's past that could do such a terrible thing—and why had he never heard of them before?

CHAPTER FOURTEEN

May 15, 1794

IT WAS RATHER difficult to walk downstairs in the large skirts of the current fashion. One was always more balanced when able to see one's feet.

But when carrying such a large number of bedsheets, it was almost impossible. Opal took each step at a time, careful not to lift one foot before the other had found a secure lodging. It would never do, after all, to tumble to the bottom and seriously hurt something.

Opal's fingers gripped the linens as Coral appeared at the bottom of the stairs.

"Is that all of them?"

Opal nodded, still concentrating on her steps. "As many as I can find. Will they do?"

Reaching the bottom step, Opal heaved a sigh of relief as her shoulders loosened and the worrisome knot at the back of her neck disappeared. She never enjoyed carrying anything downstairs; it was one of the reasons she was certain all three of her children had learned to walk so quickly. If they wanted to follow their Mama downstairs and not take a tumble, they had to be steady on their feet.

Coral looked carefully at the sheets in her mother's hands

with a serious expression, a little puckering frown on her face. Opal was careful to keep her smile just under the surface.

She had never believed she would birth and raise a daughter so serious as Coral. In a way, it was a blessing. One day she would be the head of the de Petras family, and she may need to make serious decisions for the betterment of her siblings and own little ones.

But the way she approached every decision or choice in life with such severity…

"I do not believe there are any more," Opal said into the silence, in the hope it would encourage her daughter to speak. "But if required, I can send Meredith to purchase more."

Coral shook her head. "No, I do not think that will be necessary."

Opal nodded solemnly. "Creating a den is a serious business."

"Are you laughing at me, Mama?" asked Coral sincerely.

It was difficult to reply with anything but a lie when her daughter put it like that, Opal mused. Really, she should treasure these moments. Coral appeared to grow another inch every time she looked.

"Only a little bit," she confessed.

Opal had readied herself for pouting from her daughter at her admission, but to her surprise, Coral smiled. "Papa laughs at me all the time."

Heart twisting with both pain and joy, Opal smiled at her daughter. *Their daughter.*

Happiness? The word could not sufficiently capture just how glorious it was now Jasper was back, all right with the world. The paperwork was almost ready, from what Mr. Cleland said, and then…then they could discuss remarriage. A small ceremony, nothing complicated. Just them and their children.

There had been such pain, such loneliness, but that time was over, never to return.

But it was moments like these that proved to Opal just how strange and difficult it had been without him—not just for herself, but for the children.

"Well, that is only something your father does to the people he truly cares for," Opal said confidentially. "You are fortunate indeed."

Coral nodded, her smile remaining. "He really does love us, doesn't he?"

Opal breathed in deeply, joy soaring through her, but before she could say anything, Jasper's voice came from the parlor, the door still open.

"Where are those sheets, Coral? This den won't build itself!"

A squeal of delight from Emerald followed Jasper's words. Opal shook her head with a laugh. There was something truly different about a father. She could have raised perfectly good children without him, she knew, but now that he was back…

"Here you go," Opal said aloud to Coral. "Take them on through."

The pile of sheets looked remarkably large in Coral's arms. Opal could only just see her daughter's eyes over the linens.

"Are you going to come to play, too?"

It was such a strange question, it made Opal pause. Play? She had never been a parent to play. She never could have been; she was the authority figure, the one who made them clear their plates or go to bed early if they had been naughty.

"Of course I will," she said softly.

Coral beamed, and Opal sighed with happiness. If only these days could continue forever, unchanging. As though she could trap this day in time and visit it whenever she wished.

"We have already made quite advancements with the den, you can see that—"

Coral's excited chatter was interrupted by the doorbell, the jangling noise echoing down the hall. Two sharp knocks followed it; clearly, Opal thought wryly, the individual outside had a matter of great import to discuss.

She looked up the hall but saw no sign of Mrs. Clarkson, the housekeeper, nor the two maids.

"—and Papa says once we have enough sheets—"

"Yes, yes," said Opal, not paying attention. "Coral, go on through."

"You said you would come through and play with us," said Coral—not accusingly exactly, but not too far removed from it.

"I did," said Opal hastily as the doorbell jangled again, "but I must see to the door."

It appeared her daughter did not need an invitation. Scampering away and entering the parlor to the cheers of her Papa, Coral was gone in an instant as a flurry of angry-sounding knocks could be heard on the front door.

Opal sighed. She really must have a conversation with Mrs. Clarkson; there were few duties of such a woman, and really, they could get by with another maid who could be far more helpful in the kitchen and with laundry.

But there was something about having a housekeeper, Opal reflected as she walked down the hall toward the front door. When one did not have a title, having a housekeeper was a sign of one's breeding, and one's suitability for one's daughters to marry a title…

Opal opened the door. A chilly breeze swept into the house, and on the steps before her stood a woman of about her age, though dressed in far shabbier clothes. There was a scowl on her face—an expression Opal could have guessed, merely based on the volume and rapidity of the knocking.

"Yes?"

The woman looked her up and down openly, no shyness in her manner. "Blimey, I ent never seen a housekeeper as fancy as you!"

Opal smiled dryly. She was not wearing her best gown. It was only a day gown of dark blue cotton, but it certainly had pretty embroidering on the bodice, and as usual, her skirts were full.

"I suppose I would be," she said wryly, "except this is my own house, I am no servant. Can I help you?"

As she asked the question, Opal wondered why the woman,

whoever she was, had not chosen to go to the servants' entrance below. There was a roughness to her appearance and an unkemptness to her apparel that suggested a lower class of woman than one Opal would expect to come to the front door.

Her hands were red, rubbed stiff in some places. A seamstress, perhaps? Perhaps she was looking for work; there were plenty of houses that required a little help on laundry day.

"I am looking," said the woman, drawing herself up as though she could hear Opal's silent disapproval, "for a Mr. Jasper de Petras."

Opal's stomach swooped painfully, as though she had missed a step while carrying the linens for Coral's den. Her lungs were tight, too tight, making every breath painful.

"I am looking for a Mr. Jasper de Petras."

Opal had never realized just how unpleasant it was to hear Jasper's name on the lips of another woman until this very moment. But it was not just hearing his name that chilled her blood. It was the fact of the woman's presence, suggestive that Jasper had not been truthful.

"I was never unfaithful to you. Never. I could not even imagine it, it-it—it would be unfathomable."

She had believed him.

He had betrayed her. He had lain with another, taken his pleasure where he could find it because he could not find it with her. And he had lied. Opal was not sure which was worse. The betrayal itself, or the lies which had attempted to conceal it.

Oh, she had been such a fool. So quick to believe Jasper, so eager to believe he had been faithful to her, that he had not even been tempted.

But seven years was a long time for a man to be abstinent, was it not?

A bitter taste tanged in her mouth. Opal swallowed, but it did not dissipate as she stared at the woman before her.

The woman was glaring. "Are you deaf?"

Opal swallowed. She needed to get a hold of herself. She was the mistress here; this was her home. She was not going to permit herself to be overwhelmed by a lightskirt who may have tupped her husband.

"No. No, I am not," she said. "You seek…Jasper de Petras."

The last three words become a whisper, but the woman did not seem to have noticed.

She nodded vigorously, going on tiptoes to look around Opal. "Is he here?"

The muffled laughter of Jasper and their children spilled out from the parlor, and Opal's heart broke. *It was all over.* The perfection she had believed they had finally found…it was gone.

"No." Her voice cracked, and Opal cleared her throat before continuing. "No. He is not here."

The lie tasted bitter on her tongue. Had it tasted as bitter to Jasper when he had lied?

The woman shook her head with a heavy sigh. "Blast. I've looked all over for 'im. He owes me money, an' all," spat the woman.

A gut-wrenching ache seared Opal's chest. "Of course he does."

"D'you know where is, then?" asked the woman hopefully. "He owes me quite a bit of money, then he just disappeared! The blaggard went missing!"

Opal closed her eyes for a moment with the pain, then opened them. "I cannot help you," she said stiffly. "But if you leave your details with my servants below, I will endeavor to have the money sent to you."

The woman gave her a rather appraising look. It was unpleasant to be viewed in such a way by anyone, but to be beheld by Jasper's harlot…it was intolerable.

"You know where he is, then?"

Jasper's laughter reached Opal's ears, and her throat became constricted, making all conversation difficult.

"I…" Opal hesitated but pushed on. "I believe in paying one's debts."

Thankfully, the woman did not appear to require any additional information. She nodded. "Tomorrow."

She had already turned away before Opal could ask her name. Not that it mattered. Perhaps it was better she did not know.

Closing the door slowly, she leaned against it and waited for the world to stop spinning. It was so fast, the giddiness almost overwhelming, she was unsure whether she would faint or vomit.

Swallowing both pride and panic, she sat on the bottom step of the staircase.

She needed to think. Needed to be away from him.

She would do what was necessary to protect her family, keep them safe from harm—from the pain that was to come, whether it was tomorrow or the day after, or years in the future. If that meant leaving Jasper behind for a time to consider what she truly wanted, then so be it.

Taking a deep breath, Opal rose to her feet, brushed her skirts, and stepped over to the parlor door. She arranged her face in a smile, hoped to God her eyes were not red with unshed tears, and opened the door.

"My goodness, you do not need my help! Look at the wonderful den you have built!"

CHAPTER FIFTEEN

May 17, 1794

"**B**UT I DO not understand," came the whine of Micah, grating on Opal's nerves like nothing else could. "Why are we going to visit Lady Romeril?"

Opal swallowed and waited for the moving carriage to traverse this particularly cumbersome piece of road, churning her insides, until she opened her mouth.

For it was a valid question. After all, the children had never met Lady Romeril. Opal had always been careful to keep her children completely separate from her attempts to move once more into the best circles of Society.

Afternoon teas, dinners, visits…she had conducted them alone.

A painful lurch in her stomach made Opal bring her handkerchief to her mouth once more. This dratted carriage; she had never felt so unwell in all her life.

But she could not lie to herself. It was not purely the rambunctious carriage churning her stomach, making it seemingly impossible to keep her hastily consumed breakfast down.

No, it was Jasper de Petras. He was a part of her past now, not her future. She should not be wasting any more time on him than was necessary.

"Mother!" Micah said sharply, pulling Admiral from the floor of the carriage onto his lap. The dog snuffled and leaned up to lick the boy's face. "Why are we visiting Lady Romeril?"

Opal wished she had an answer—at least, one she could share. She had always promised herself that she would be open with her children.

Honest as her own family never had been.

But that was before life had become complicated. Opal had been determined to get out of the house before Jasper realized what her preparations the last few days had meant, get out of London and into the countryside. Then she would afford herself time to consider.

"Perhaps," piped up Coral, seated opposite Opal and beside her brother, "we cannot afford our house anymore, and so Mama has decided to live with Lady Romeril to save money. Is that true, Mama? Are we destitute?"

Despite her misery, Opal could not help but smile at the strange pronouncement from her eldest child. Really, wherever had Coral got such a strange idea about their wealth and financial affairs?

In a few years, she would begin her training. Coral was almost old enough to have a view of the household accounts, the day-to-day running of a home. She would need to learn how to manage not only a household but a family. Then she would see just how "destitute" the de Petras family really was…

"Coral de Petras, you do have the most strange ideas," Opal said mildly. "We certainly do not need to vacate our house, there are no concerns in that quarter whatsoever. It is just…"

Opal hesitated, the words she was considering sounding rather flat in her mind. There was just no point in trying to give a reasonable explanation. What could she say? *Your father has betrayed me for the last time, and I needed to get away to consider what to do next?*

"I thought," Opal said firmly, "it would be pleasant for you to visit with Lady Romeril, and Lord Romeril I suppose, and spend some time with her sons. Make some friends."

The reactions were instantaneous, and if Opal had been a gambling sort of woman, she could have put money on them.

Micah scrunched his nose as though he could already feel the frustration of having to associate with boys he had never met.

Emerald was more direct. "Boys stink."

Opal did not laugh, but it was a close call. Well, she had always hoped for daughters with a little ferocity, and Emerald was certainly shaping up to be just that, even if her nervousness in crowds meant the world had not yet seen it. She would go far with that sort of attitude. She may not be very popular while doing it...

"Boys do not stink," said Opal severely as the carriage rumbled around a corner, sliding them all to the left and then back again. "At least, not all of them, anyway. Your brother does not stink."

The moment the words left her mouth, Opal saw the trap that she had inadvertently laid for herself and sighed heavily as she watched the ensuing argument.

Her youngest glanced at Micah, who immediately stuck his tongue out and made a silly face. Emerald burst into tears.

"Micah made a face at me, and the face is horrible and it's stinky and the faaaace..."

Opal sighed. "Coral, would you be a dear and switch places with your brother," she said, grasping at the only method that she could use to quell the fight as they rattled along in a carriage.

That was the trouble with travel. When things went wrong, one had little recourse for improvement.

Coral sighed as she rose in the juddering carriage, carefully took a step as Micah picked up an unprotesting Admiral, slid behind her to where she had been sitting far from Emerald, then sat opposite her little sister.

"I hate being the eldest," she muttered.

Opal spoke without thinking. She was tired, the last few days a struggle to keep her temper and her tears at bay, every moment thinking Jasper would recognize the signs of an escape and prevent her from leaving. The words just slipped out.

"Me, too, dear."

Guilt rushed through her veins as the words seemed to echo around the carriage. She had promised herself before Coral had even been born, that she would never speak of her past with the children. Or with Jasper. Oh, he had met her mother, but that was all. That was enough.

The carriage shuddered slightly, then its pace changed. It was slowing.

"Are we there?" Micah asked eagerly, looking out of the carriage window. "Are we at Lady Romeril's house?"

"And Lord Romeril's house," Opal corrected.

Really, that was perhaps the most difficult thing she was going to have to navigate. Her children had been raised in a household where she was the head. It was no surprise, in hindsight, that it appeared they believed every household was the same.

The drive was not overly long, and before long, the carriage pulled up. Opal let out a deep breath.

"But Mama," said Coral with a heavy sigh, "you don't even like Lady Romeril."

"Hush child!" Opal glanced at the two footmen stepping toward the carriage. The last thing she needed was for them to take an ill report of her to their mistress. Her cheeks tinged slightly with the lie as she continued, "I like Lady Romeril, of course, I do."

Deciding what to do next would be crucial, something she could not rush.

Coral was right, though. If Opal had had any other options, she would certainly have gone to them instead of Lady Romeril, but then her re-entrance into Society had been so recent. There were few ladies, in truth, who Opal could go to at all.

Gentlemen, on the other hand...

If she truly had been a widow, she would have had a lover by now, a gentleman on whom she could have relied in any situation of difficulty—though admittedly, one's husband reemerging from the grave would have scuppered that.

With no other friends, Opal had no choice. Lady Romeril was her only option.

"M'lady," murmured a footman as he opened the door to the carriage and proffered a hand. "Lady Romeril welcomes you."

The words were said stiffly, but Opal attempted not to notice as she graciously accepted the hand and was helped out of the carriage. It may just be the footman's way, after all. It did not necessarily speak directly to the temperament of her hostess.

"Lady Romeril welcomes us?" repeated Micah, sticking his head out of the carriage cheekily, Admiral poking his snout out and sniffing the air. "Well, where is she then?"

"Micah de Petras, hold your tongue," Opal said quickly. "Come on."

It took a few moments to help all three of her children out of the carriage. Coral refused the hands offered to her by both mother and footman and stumbled as she came out of the coach, caught by Opal who said nothing. Coral stood by with red cheeks as Micah accepted his mother's hand and ignored the footman, and Emerald cried, refused to come out, and had to be lifted bodily from the carriage.

Well, this was not precisely how she had expected to arrive, Opal thought wearily as she carried the heavy, sobbing weight of her youngest child. But there it was. They were here.

The large house before them was impressive, built in the new style with a delicate symmetry. Lady Romeril's estate—*Lord Romeril's estate*, Opal corrected silently—was sufficiently far from London to prevent anyone from accidentally coming upon her, and she would have to hope Jasper would not know of it.

Returning to Italy was out of the question, not after... Bath was also impossible. It was the first place Jasper would look. Perhaps the north? No, not after that wonderful moment they had shared reminiscing about the Lake District, the closeness they had—

"Ah, Mrs. de Petras, how...interesting."

Opal took a deep breath, plastered a smile on her lips, and

tried her best to curtesy with a heavy child in her arms. "Lady Romeril."

Lady Romeril had descended the steps and moved toward them, arms open and an expressive, cheerful look on her face. "So wonderful of you to invite yourself and your children to my country house for…how long did you say it was?"

It was all Opal could do not to laugh. Well, she had to hand it to the woman. Lady Romeril really did have a way with words.

"And these are your children, I suppose," said Lady Romeril, halting just before them and examining Coral, Micah, and finally, Emerald. "And a dog, my word. If they go into the hallway, my butler is waiting for them. He will show them the way to the kitchen where I have given instructions that they can eat anything they like."

Micah did not need further invitation. Without a backward glance at his mother, he raced forward into the house, Admiral scampering at his heels.

Emerald immediately stopped crying. "Anything?"

Lady Romeril peered into the red eyes and puffy cheeks of the child in Opal's arms. "Anything."

Opal allowed her littlest to slip from her arms and follow her brother.

Coral looked at her mother for permission. "May I, Mama?"

Pride swelled in Opal's chest. "Of course, off you go."

While it was obvious Coral wished to demonstrate that she, the eldest, was far more restrained, the idea of eating absolutely anything in Lady Romeril's kitchen proved too much. By the time she reached the door, she was running.

"What delightful children."

Opal swelled with pride. "Yes, I think so."

"What a pity," Lady Romeril said delicately, "that you are committed to the strangest of ideas. Letting Coral inherit, for example."

Perhaps it was the stress and strain of the last few days; perhaps it was her own argumentative nature suppressed for too long.

But Opal found herself speaking far more directly to Lady Romeril than she had ever spoken to anyone in polite Society before. "Yes. Coral will inherit, and what's more Lady Romeril, both she and Emerald will not only keep their names when they marry, but their husbands will take ours. I believe I have mentioned this before, and it is not something I am ashamed of. Do you think I should be?"

There was genuine surprise on the face of her hostess, but she was not easily provoked.

"My, my, so much I have to learn about you, Mrs. de Petras," Lady Romeril said silkily. "Won't you come in? And your husband, or late husband, I am not entirely sure still how to address him. What a delightful man you have—why does he linger in the coach?"

Agonizing guilt stabbed Opal's heart. When would he realize that they were gone? How long would he wait for them to return from some outing and then realize, slowly, they were not returning?

Perhaps she should have left a note.

She would have to go missing just as he had gone missing all those years ago. Opal had no choice. She would not allow him to hurt the children or most importantly, her heart.

"Mrs. de Petras?"

Opal smiled at the waiting Lady Romeril. "Shall we go in?"

If Lady Romeril had been surprised at her complete refusal to answer the question about her husband, she did not show it. The minute it took them to cross the driveway, ascend the steps, and enter the hallway gave Opal just enough possession of herself to speak calmly again.

"Sadly, Jasper was detained in town."

"Oh, no matter," said Lady Romeril breezily. "I will make sure one of my footmen sends a note round to let him know that he can come any time he—"

"No!" Opal flushed as the word echoed around the hallway. She should not have been so swift, so decisive.

A smile crept across Lady Romeril's face. "Oh, so it's like that, is it?"

If only she'd had the presence of mind to say something else—something calm and seemingly off the cuff. Opal should have considered this, should have planned for some sort of excuse in the carriage.

If only the children had given her space to think…

But the very idea of Jasper finding her so soon sent panic roaring through her veins.

Opal sighed, her shoulders sagging. "I come to you for help, Lady Romeril. Surely you will not hold it against me?"

Lady Romeril smiled. "My dear, whether you are running from your husband or not, none of that is my concern. I just need to be the center of the action. You may stay as long as you want."

Perhaps she had underestimated Lady Romeril. In a very real way, she was the closest thing to an Englishwoman like her—the queen of her own castle.

"Thank you," Opal said honestly. "I…I am grateful."

Lady Romeril replied, saying something that Opal could not quite make out. Her mind had been overwhelmed with the memory of that woman who had turned up at her door, demanding money—demanding it of Jasper.

"He owes me quite a bit of money, then he just disappeared!"

Opal forced a smile on her face as Lady Romeril chattered on. She could not think on that now. She had done what she had always done—what was right for her children.

Just as she thought of them, the children reappeared, clutching marchpane and accompanied by two boys who must be Lady Romeril's sons.

"Mama, look!" said Emerald, holding up the marchpane, sticky sweetness all around her mouth.

"We should save some for Father," said Micah eagerly, looking at his mother with a wide smile. "Where is he?"

"I have no idea," said Opal harshly, unable to prevent bitterness from seeping through.

CHAPTER SIXTEEN

May 20, 1794

J ASPER POUNDED HEAVILY on the door.

He regretted it at once. It echoed loudly in the darkness, but it was absolute murder on the knuckles. Lifting his hand to his mouth and sucking on his sore fingers, Jasper pulled at the doorbell chain once again and heard it rattle.

They must be able to hear him. It was impossible that there was not a single servant about the place, even at this time—and it couldn't be that late—who could open the door. Which meant that they had been instructed not to open the door. Was that it?

Wild thoughts tumbled through Jasper's mind as he removed his hand from his mouth and started hammering at the door again.

"Open up!"

The slight drizzle which he had ignored when he had started out on his journey had increased now. Raindrops dripped down the back of his neck, chilling Jasper to the bone, despite the earlier warmth of the day.

His collar was soaked. Jasper could feel the cold seeping into his skin as he stood, battling against a door that would not open. He would wait here, rain or no rain, until they opened this damn door.

"Open up, I say!" Jasper called out, his voice hoarse. Exhaustion tugged at the corners of his eyes, but he refused to go back home.

How could he call that place home if Opal and the children were not there?

A dark shadow had entered his soul the moment he realized they had gone. This was the only place they could be. There was nowhere else.

And once they bothered to open the door, he would force his way in and make Opal show him whatever letter had arrived to frighten her off.

The wind blew, a rumble of thunder threatened a greater storm to come, but Jasper ignored it. He was cold, wet, and alone. How much worse could things get?

Do not think on it, Jasper told himself darkly. He did not need to invite God to show him any more pain or misery.

Jasper bashed his fist painfully against the door again. "Damn it all, let me in!"

Whether it was the amount of time he had waited, whether his knocking had become particularly violent, or whether his cry of desperation had shifted the hearts of those inside, Jasper did not know.

He was suddenly blinded as the door opened and a footman appeared holding a candle. "I am afraid my master is not receiving guests at this time, so—sir, I say!"

Jasper did not say a word. By the time he had pushed rudely past the footman, stomped into the hallway, and adjusted to the dim light, he was beyond all expected niceties.

"Maltravers!"

A little late for visitors, to be sure, but their friendship went so far back that there was surely no time he could not arrive here.

"Goodness!"

Jasper whirled around to look at the man who had appeared in a doorway.

"Good God," said the Earl of Maltravers in a hushed voice.

"What are you doing here at this hour, de Petras?"

Jasper stared at his friend and suddenly became conscious of what he was doing and where he was. He was standing on a rather fine rug—an Axminster if he was not mistaken—dripping a great deal of water onto it. His boots were muddy, and the silt of the road was gently soaking into the rug. It was late—far later than he had imagined. Later than it was polite to receive guests.

Ah. Perhaps he should have thought about this a little more before rushing off to the one man he had been certain would be protecting Opal. But where else would she go?

"It…" Jasper swallowed, then said blankly, "Is it late?"

Maltravers approached him with a great look of concern. "If I was any judge, man, I would say that you have seen a ghost. What has happened?"

"A ghost of a man, perhaps," Jasper said bitterly. "I see him when I examine myself in a looking glass—you do not happen to have any dry clothes I can borrow, do you?"

His voice had fallen, becoming a little apologetic. One did not generally pound down a friend's front door as though the very hounds of hell were at your heels if you did not have a good enough reason, and "Opal left me" did not feel quite enough.

Jasper swallowed. It was bad enough to have one's woman disappear, but to go begging to a friend for dry clothes because you took neither the precaution of a greatcoat nor the sensible idea of taking a carriage…

Perhaps he needed more sleep. Perhaps that was it.

Maltravers's face was still concerned, but a small smile had appeared on his face. "For you? Of course. My footman will show you the way to my dressing room, take whatever will fit—but do be quiet, for heaven's sake! James is asleep up there, or at least he was. You've made enough of a ruckus to wake the entire household."

Jasper's heart twisted, ripples of agony combining to create a painful harmony within his chest. James, of course. It had been years since he had seen the boy—why, he must be eight, nine years old?

James was upstairs in bed, warm and safe, and his father knew precisely where he was. But where was Micah? Was he warm and safe?

But he could not speak these fears aloud, not yet. Jasper followed the footman upstairs, the single candlestick in the servant's hand sufficient to show the way. The dressing room was just off the main bedchamber, but it had its own door onto the landing, and after the footman had bowed him in, he thrust a towel into the unwelcome guest's arms, handed him the candlestick, and left him to it.

It took but ten minutes for Jasper to entirely strip off his sodden clothes, leaving them in a pile on the floor—better that than a chair, he guessed—and rummage through his friend's clothes to see what he could find.

Thankfully, they were much of a size, and so it did not take him long to find breeches, shirt, and waistcoat that would do. Maltravers favored a far more flamboyant style, Jasper thought wryly as he caught a glimpse of himself in a full-length mirror. Far more embroidery and ruffles than was good for a man.

Still, he was grateful and knew he did not deserve such hospitality after barreling into the man's house in the dead of night for no good cause. It was clear Opal was not here; the townhouse was small, and there were few places where four people could be hidden. Maltravers had not seemed concerned that he had arrived. There were no secrets here.

The children would be asleep by now, Jasper thought with misery seeping into his heart. But where? Were they comfortable? Did they miss him?

A creak downstairs. Maltravers was still awake then. Jasper rubbed at his eyes, glancing quickly at his sore knuckles that were scraped and slightly bleeding. He must be polite; he could not merely ensconce himself in his friend's dressing room and refuse to talk to him.

When Jasper reached the hallway, he approached the door

from whence Maltravers had appeared and opened it to reveal a drawing room. His friend was seated with a glass of wine in his hand and a book in the other.

A smile crept across the earl's face as Jasper closed the door. "Better?"

"Dryer, certainly," said Jasper shortly. He would make polite conversation for a few minutes, try to find out whether Maltravers knew anything about Opal's disappearance, then either collapse into sleep here or find his way back to the house.

"Can I get you a glass?" asked Maltravers, lifting his half-drunk glass of wine.

"A large one," Jasper said heavily as he dropped into an armchair by the fire. The flickering flames started to warm his cold bones, and he shivered, gazing into the fire.

"There may be…someone. A someone in my past."

The memory surfaced slowly, but it shook Jasper to his core. He had barely picked up on Opal's words when she had first spoken, but now in hindsight, he should have sent away the children and encouraged her to tell him everything she suspected.

She knew—or at the very least, she had an idea who the letter writer could be. He should have asked her, made her tell him what this was all about. Opal had had an inkling, but he had not pressed her. He should have done. That was his own fault.

A glass of wine appeared before him. "It is about time you showed up, you know. I was beginning to worry."

Jasper blinked as he took the glass of wine, his mind struggling to understand what had been said. But questions could wait. Wine first.

The potency of the red wine flared his mind to life, and Jasper sighed as the liquid began to warm him from the inside out.

"What do you mean, worry?" he asked finally, after half of the wine was gone.

Was it possible—a stray thought meandered through his mind, but Jasper clung to it, desperate to find meaning in what had occurred. Did Maltravers mean he knew where Opal had gone? Had she perhaps told him, as a failsafe in case something terrible happened to her?

Jasper leaned forward, eagerly staring at his friend who had taken the seat opposite him. "You know where she is, don't you?"

He saw the answer the moment the words had left his lips. Maltravers blinked, clearly confused, not comprehending the fragment of the sentence Jasper had uttered.

"Where she is? What on earth do you mean?"

Jasper's heart sank. *Well, he supposed that would have been too easy.*

"No, I wanted to hear the full story from you," said Maltravers, lifting his refreshed glass of wine in a silent toast to his friend. "Now there's been a happy ending. I assume my invitation to your second wedding is in the post or mislaid—it cannot be long, surely? The gossip around town is that Mr. Cleland must have finished the paperwork by now."

Sinking back into the chair, Jasper could not have believed he would have felt worse than when he first entered this house, but he did now. All glimmers of hope were gone. This had been the only place he could think of left to try, the only real friend to the de Petras family, and it was a false trail.

Maltravers clearly had no clue where Opal was—he did not even seem to know she had been misplaced.

"Now there's been a happy ending."

He could think of no unhappier ending than Opal going missing, and with Coral, Micah, and Emerald, too.

Jasper sighed heavily. "There is no happy ending. Opal's gone."

He looked up to see his friend's response, with the slightest hope he may have heard something in the gossip mill.

But Maltravers looked absolutely horrified. "But—but surely you were to be married again? What do you mean, gone?"

Jasper sipped at his wine again. It would not do to finish the entire glass so quickly; he had not eaten after all, and he did not wish to be obnoxious. "I woke one morning, and she was gone."

Was there any other way to explain it? Jasper could see no way of dressing it up into any fancier language. Opal was missing.

Maltravers looked at him carefully, then put down his wine. "Well, this won't do."

Getting up, he walked back to his drinks cabinet, pulled out two brandy glasses, and a nearly full bottle of brandy.

When the earl returned to the fireplace, he thrust out a glass to Jasper. "Here."

Jasper took it without question and held it out—but Maltravers poured himself a glass first, then handed the entire bottle to his guest.

After sitting heavily, Maltravers took a sip of his brandy, then fixed his friend with a sharp look. "Now, I am going to speak plainly to you, as I hope an old friend like you would do for me. Do you blame her?"

It was a reasonable question, that was the worst part. "No," said Jasper with a sigh, pouring a large measure of the brandy into his glass. "At least, if she left of her own free will. I suppose she is completely within her right to abandon me, as I abandoned her."

As he spoke the words, pain tightened his chest. Was that perhaps what had happened? Not that a terrible letter had arrived, putting them all in danger—but had Opal eventually realized a life without him was preferable to one with him?

"You never did explain to me why you took off, by the way," Maltravers said mildly. "With my wife gone, I couldn't think of abandoning James, obviously, though I am sure you had your reasons..."

His voice trailed off, but Jasper smiled wryly. "I admire your self-restraint. Obviously, you think I was a cad."

"A complete fool," said his friend cheerfully, but then he continued a little more seriously. "But I know you better than that. You must have had a reason, even if it is not one I would understand or necessarily agree with. What was it?"

Jasper sighed. It all seemed so long ago. "We received threatening letters—I received them, anyway. Quite brutal threats against the children, against Opal, and the order to leave them to protect them. Who could we go to? No knowledge of who sent them, no recourse for justice against an unknown threat…"

Maltravers whistled slowly. "So…you were told to leave by a stranger?"

"I know it may sound ridiculous, and perhaps it was in hindsight," Jasper admitted. "But at the time, I was convinced it was the only way to protect them. I was younger then."

"Stupider."

Jasper took another swig of brandy. Its searing heat seemed to revive him, but nothing could truly awaken his heart now that he had lost the only people who truly mattered to him.

"But that is neither here nor there," said Maltravers bracingly. "The question is, what changed? When you returned, I mean. Why did she off and leave you?"

Jasper winced, but he supposed that was the long and short of it. "We were getting on so well, as a husband and wife ought to, if you…know what I mean."

The earl raised an eyebrow but said nothing.

"And then a few days ago…gone."

"With the children?" asked his friend quietly.

A lump rose in Jasper's throat, and he found he could not speak. Saying it aloud somehow would mean it true in a way that nothing else had. He nodded.

Maltravers sighed heavily, and the two men sat in silence for a few minutes, watching the fire and sipping their brandy.

"Well, if you want her back—"

"Of course I want her back!" Jasper said, outraged. *The very idea he could live the rest of his life without her…madness!*

Maltravers raised his hands in mock surrender. "A man doesn't like to assume! Well, if you want her back—"

His words were interrupted by a commotion in the hallway. A ruckus, not unlike the noise Jasper himself had raised in demanding entrance.

The earl sighed wearily. "For goodness' sake, what now? I

thought you would be my last uninvited guest this evening."

There was a voice raised in the hall—a voice that Jasper recognized, though he could not place it. The footman was arguing, and the volume of their voices rose.

"No, you cannot go in there—madam!"

The door was flung open, and there stood Mrs. Norton.

Jasper rose to his feet, astonished. "Mrs. Norton!"

What on earth was she doing here? It made no sense. Mrs. Norton, here, of all places?

Maltravers looked vaguely between the two of them. "You know this woman?"

But before Jasper could explain, Mrs. Norton strode forward and glared most furiously at Jasper. "There you are!"

"Yes, I know her," said Jasper hastily. "She was my landlady for a short while when—"

"I have tracked you down, at last, you blaggard, and in the house of an earl no less!" Mrs. Norton said over him. "I want my money! You owe me sixteen shillings, you thief, and if the woman at the house won't give it to me, then you must!"

Jasper shook his head, utterly bewildered. "Woman at the house? What do you..."

And then it all became clear to him. Woman at the—Opal. She must have met Mrs. Norton, and a great misunderstanding must have occurred. If his old landlady had appeared demanding money yet not given any context to which the debt had been created...

Jasper swallowed. *Oh, dear God. She must have thought...Opal must have believed him unfaithful—that Mrs. Norton was some sort of harlot!*

The idea would be rather funny if it were not so serious.

So, there had been no more threatening letters. It was Opal alone who had decided to disappear from his life.

"—and even with you gone, I knew I'd track you down and make you pay—"

"For the love of all things holy, pay the woman, Maltravers," said Jasper distractedly, hardly able to think with that woman's shouting. "My coin is elsewhere, I will repay you."

Maltravers said nothing, for which Jasper was eternally grateful. After giving the woman a pound note, which made her eyes widen and her mouth mercifully shut, Jasper paced across the room and opened the door.

"Mrs. Norton is leaving," he said sharply to the footman.

Jasper slammed the door behind her and then turned to his friend. In the intervening time, something that had not quite made sense at the time was starting to echo in his mind.

"Well, if you want her back…"

Why would Maltravers had said such a thing…unless…

"You know where she is, don't you?" Jasper did not intend to speak so sharply, but he had to know—and the instant he spoke, he could see the truth in his face. "Maltravers!"

"I do not *know*, per se," said the earl hastily.

Jasper rolled his eyes. "You must at least have a guess. Society must be full of gossip!"

Maltravers sighed. "If I did, and it is only a guess mark you, should I tell you?"

It was not the response he had expected, but it was a fair one. Jasper hesitated, wondering precisely how he could explain to his old friend just what he had suffered these last few days, being apart from her. From them.

"You wouldn't want to be separated from your boy, would you?"

"James?" Maltravers shook his head. "Not unless I deserved it."

It was an excellent response, and in Jasper's tiredness, he barely knew whether he deserved to find his family again or not. Was he the perfect husband? Was he the perfect father? Did he deserve a third chance to become those things?

"I may not deserve Opal," Jasper said finally with a hint of despair, "but I love her. I want to deserve her."

Maltravers smiled. "That is all I needed to hear."

Chapter Seventeen

May 21, 1794

Inching her hand ever so carefully to her mouth, Opal was careful to yawn behind it, clenching her jaw as much as possible. It would not do to be rude.

There. The instinct to yawn was forced down, and Opal congratulated herself silently on managing, once again, to prevent her hostess from seeing just how incredibly dull she found the entire conversation.

"...but, of course, the last time I saw him, I told him, I said you simply have to stop doing that my dear man, 'tis most unseemly! He was rather astonished if truth be told, but he was so enamored with me as a youth—did I ever tell you that story? Oh, 'tis a marvelous one. It all began..."

Or was it perhaps a form of torture, Opal mused as she tried to nod at the right times in the plentiful stories she was being "entertained" with. Perhaps Lady Romeril was a military weapon. Perhaps they could put her to good use in France.

Or was her hostess in fact attempting to force Opal to leave? She had not been here that long, and Opal was certain Lady Romeril was far more interested in the potential for scandal than the trouble of a few houseguests. At least, that was what she had said the first night they had been here, at dinner.

"My dear Mrs. de Petras," Lady Romeril had said smoothly, "if you believe you can escape your husband while simultaneously escaping scandal, I am very sorry to inform you that you are quite mistaken. Don't you think, Lord Romeril?"

"Hmmph?" Lord Romeril had started, almost asleep at the other end of the dining table.

"You see?" Lady Romeril had pointed a fork at her husband smugly as if that proved it. "He agrees."

But that had been days ago. Opal tried to focus on what Lady Romeril was saying now.

"—best godson any woman could have hoped for! Yes, he is still young, but I believe young Braedon has great promise. Why, I even think that one day he will make an excellent husband, though what lady will take on that man...and my sons are far better prospects, do not you think?"

Opal nodded. It appeared she was not actually required to say anything. She reached down and patted Admiral who was snoozing on her feet.

"Yes, the best of sons, though I admit I would like a daughter. You have two, and that is all very well, but only one son of course. *My* two boys..."

Opal's gaze drifted to the garden where the five children were collected on the lawn. The footmen had placed a medley of blankets out there for them, and as far as she could see—though she could not hear them—they appeared content.

A rueful smile crept across her lips. Would her children blame her, one day, for taking them away from their father? Gone without a word to him, or them, about why?

"—quite the cleverest boys of their age, and I simply must get a governess for them—though it is so hard to find one of repute, do you not think? If only there was some sort of...I do not know, a bureau of some sort that could provide references. You must find the same with your children, though none are as intelligent as my boys. Why, only yesterday, one of them said to me..."

Opal nodded vaguely, giving Lady Romeril's words no heed.

"I hope I am not boring you, Mrs. de Petras," Lady Romeril said tartly.

Stifling a yawn and hoping beyond hope her hostess would not notice, Opal smiled. "Oh, no, not bored at all. Absolutely fascinating, the whole thing. Do continue."

Lady Romeril examined her closely for a moment, but only a moment. Evidently, it was far more pleasant to have an audience than not, even if that audience may be a little tired.

The more she permitted herself to think about Jasper—and she was doing her best not to permit it, but the damned handsome man kept intruding into her thoughts—the more Opal wondered whether she had done the right thing.

Opal did not like the thought, but it continued to interfere with her thinking, continuously prodding into her mind. After all, she had criticized Jasper—not without cause—for not speaking to her about the threatening letters when they had arrived. He had kept them to himself, worried about them himself, then taken an action she certainly would not have advised if they had had the chance to discuss it together…

And what had she done the moment something arose that made her doubt him?

Opal shifted uncomfortably in her seat. Why, she had done precisely what she had berated Jasper for doing in the first place.

"…such clever boys," Lady Romeril said fondly. "I do believe they are even more advanced than your Micah, though they be a few years younger."

Opal had to smile, though it was a mirthless one. "I suppose every mother thinks their son is the most impressive, the most intelligent. That is what makes us their mothers."

Lady Romeril smiled. "Yes, I quite agree, Mrs. de Petras. I mean to say, what woman would be good enough for a Romeril?" she asked tartly. "I have to say I am raising them to have a very good opinion of themselves, and quite rightly, too. When one thinks about…"

A memory infringed on Opal's calm mind.

"Well, if not someone from Italy, then who? Who would want to see us apart, separate and alone?"

Opal's stomach contracted painfully, then relaxed. Their most common topic of conversation, of course, were the threatening letters, though she had managed to avoid giving her definite opinion.

Perhaps, as a hint of regret tinged her thoughts, she should have told Jasper of her suspicions.

After all, it could easily have been her brother who wrote them, Opal thought darkly. She would not put it past him, and though she had left Italy all those years ago as a newly wedded bride, she had been certain to travel far enough away to put all that behind her.

A shout—something penetrated the glass of the Orangery. Opal looked up, neck and shoulders tight, but as her gaze fell upon the children, she could see they were quite happily playing. It was a scream of delight, not fear.

She sank back in her chair and tried not to permit her panic to rise. Yes, she had been so arrogant as to assume that her brother would never follow her here. That she was safe. That they all were.

But what if she wasn't? What if, at the end of the day, it was *her* past that had brought this misery upon the family?

Opal sighed. She should have told him, at least her suspicions. Jasper was her husband, a piece of paper could not refute the sense in her heart, and she was supposed to trust him—but how could she, when she was finding it so difficult to trust him merely to stay faithful to her, the very basis of marriage?

"D'you know where is, then? He owes me quite a bit of money, then he just disappeared! The blaggard went missing!"

A shiver of pain moved up her side, and Opal shifted once again in her chair.

"...when one has made an alliance, of course, one's entire family gets involved," Lady Romeril was saying airily. "This is why matches are so difficult, of course. One does not marry an individual, one marries a family."

Opal nodded vaguely.

"You are thinking about that cad again, aren't you?"

Opal blinked. She had not really been paying any sort of attention to her hostess for a good few minutes now, but the sharpness of the question demanded her focus.

"I beg your pardon?"

Lady Romeril sighed and rose from her seat, meandering around the Orangery. It was a beautiful room, so broad, a part of it curved around the house, giving Lady Romeril a view from where she now stood of the drive.

"You are thinking about that man again."

Opal swallowed. "What man?"

She was not going to be drawn into a conversation about Jasper if she could help it.

It appeared she could not help it. "That odious man you have the misfortune of being married to."

Anger rose within Opal. It was all very well for her to say and think such terrible things about Jasper, but she had been his wife—she had the right to do so!

But Lady Romeril had no right, no right at all.

"Do not speak of him that way," Opal said with fury just lying under the surface of each one of her words. "I will thank you to cease speaking of him at all."

Where did this anger come from? Much of it, Opal supposed, as she felt the rush of rage surge through to her fingertips, came from being angry with Jasper himself.

Lady Romeril sniffed. "I can say what I like."

Oh, dratted woman. How she did try Opal's patience. Her Italian temper, one she had trained and hidden in this stiff and polite English Society, rose triumphantly as though rejoicing that it was finally called upon.

"I would prefer it if you didn't speak of Jasper in that way," said Opal icily. "He may not be perfect, but in most respects, he is a good man."

Lady Romeril raised an eyebrow. "My dear woman, if he is so wonderful, why are you here, hiding from him?"

It was an excellent question, one Opal was unwilling to answer. The hurt she had experienced when that woman turned up on her doorstep…it was not to be borne.

"He had his chance," Opal found herself saying bitterly, knowing she should not be so open with Lady Romeril. "Two of them. My misplaced husband cannot just turn up and expect everything to be the same."

So why did her heart rebel at her words? A part of her, and it was a growing part, was disappointed Jasper had not found them. Had he not looked? Had he not wanted to find her? Or had he just gone back to the arms of that woman?

Opal did not understand herself and certainly did not understand Jasper. She just knew she loved him. A desperate, dark love that hated to be betrayed, and yet knew that if she had not left, she would have permitted Jasper to lie to her again and again, just to have him in her life. Just to be loved in a small way by him.

"You should remember that."

Opal blinked. "I beg your pardon?"

"That he cannot just turn up and expect everything to be the same," Lady Romeril said, turning from the window.

The woman made no sense. "Why?"

"Because," Lady Romeril said with a triumphant smile, "he is knocking rather loudly on my front door."

CHAPTER EIGHTEEN

*T*HUMP, THUMP, THUMP…

By Jove, his knuckles hurt. Jasper had given them no time to heal after his frantic demands to enter Maltravers's home. He had almost rushed off that moment, in the middle of the night, to the Romerils.

But Maltravers had slowed him down. Reasoned with him. Told him his sudden appearance in the dead of night was unlikely to endear him to neither his wife nor her hosts.

Still. Jasper had not seen any reason why he could not jump on a horse as soon as daylight broke and ride hard to the Romerils' country house. And so he did, Maltravers's dire warnings that he would disturb them at breakfast ringing in his ears.

As it was, Jasper had managed to get himself entirely lost in the English countryside he did not know, and it was likely after luncheon—a meal he had not himself had—that he had found the right place.

At least, he was almost certain it was the right place. The building matched the hasty description Maltravers had given him, in any case, and Jasper barely cared about anything else. He would knock on this door as though his life depended on it— because it did.

"Opal!"

He had not intended to shout her name, but it poured out of him, a natural expression of his desperation. She was in there. As though Jasper could sense her presence. The hackles on the back of his neck had risen, and he knew, beyond anything, that she was inside.

"Open the door," Jasper shouted at the top of his lungs.

There were plenty of couples—more in the nobility than the gentry, but still—who remained wed but lived apart. It was a sorry business indeed, but then they had not been love matches. Not like himself and Opal.

"Opal," Jasper muttered, still banging loudly on the door.

Nothing happened. No footman, no window opening above him instructing him to go away, nothing. Jasper was not sure what he had expected, other than someone opening the door, and now they had not…

Jasper's stomach lurched painfully. *His children were in there.*

A strange sort of obsessive desperation overcame him, and Jasper kicked at the door, this pathetic two inches of wood that separated him from his children.

He received a sore toe for his troubles and little else. The door remained immovable, and no one came out to the front of the house to see what this strange madman wanted.

"Opal!" Jasper cried, banging on the door again, wishing there was a way to make her come out. *What could he say to provoke her…* "Micah! Coral, Emerald, are you in there?"

The door opened so suddenly that Jasper stepped backward unconsciously, as though he would need to make way for someone to leave the house. The mere glimpse of a gown, wide skirts, and embroidered bodice, and he smiled, relief washing over his soul.

She was here. His Opal.

When the door was fully opened, Jasper's face fell, and the joy that had momentarily overwhelmed him disappeared in frosty silence.

It was not Opal as he had supposed. It was Lady Romeril.

Jasper took another step back. There were few people he would wish to antagonize, and Lady Romeril was someone he would prefer to avoid at all costs.

"Where is Opal?" Jasper asked quickly.

Lady Romeril smiled imperiously. "What, no polite greeting? No good afternoon or favorable wishes regarding my health?"

Jasper worked hard to get control of his temper, fiery tendrils curling around his heart. It would not do to shout at this woman, regardless of whether she had Opal and children hidden in that house.

Jasper took a deep, calming breath. "I mean no rudeness, Lady Romeril."

"And yet," she said pleasantly, "here we are."

She pointed elegantly at her front door. Jasper's gaze moved and saw with an uncomfortable twist of his stomach a rather prominent boot print where he had kicked it.

Heat seared his face. "Not one of my finer moments."

"Obviously," said Lady Romeril dryly. "I was going to ask my butler to open the door, but after such a ruckus on my front steps, I could not permit him to step into harm's way."

She could not have said anything more calculated to make him feel like a fool. Jasper's heart sank, her depiction of him most unflattering.

"Is Opal here?" Jasper asked urgently.

Lady Romeril did not reply immediately, and Jasper examined her closely as though he could divine the answer from her face, but there was such an expression of sardonic humor there that it was quite impossible.

"What a question, Mr. de Petras," she said finally with a smirk.

Jasper snorted with irritation. "Do not give me that, I am sure she is here. Is she well? Is she safe, and the children?"

They were perfectly natural questions in Jasper's mind, questions any reasonable husband would ask after his family up and disappeared, going missing for several days.

But Lady Romeril appeared to be genuinely surprised. Her eyebrows raised, but with none of the teasing humor that he had come to expect.

"You do surprise me, Mr. de Petras," said Lady Romeril quietly.

"How delightful for me," he said dryly. "Now, is Opal with you? I wish to see her."

For a heartbeat, Jasper was certain she was going to permit him to enter, to bring him into a parlor, or drawing room, or something—and there Opal would be, the children playing at her feet. She would be confused, of course, to see him, but he would instantly put all her fears to rest, and they could be happy together, for the rest of their lives...

Instead, Lady Romeril looked Jasper up and down rather slowly, and then said icily, "Does your wife wish to see you?"

"Yes," was what Jasper wanted to say firmly. He wanted to be sure, to know for definite that his presence was not only warmly welcomed by Opal but desired.

But he could not say that. Not with the uncertainty rushing around his mind; not with Maltravers' own words echoing in his mind.

"If I did, and it is only a guess, mark you, should I tell you?"

Jasper swallowed. "I...I do not know. I do not deserve her, I know that. I do not think I ever truly deserved her in the first place, not really—but I was fortunate enough to have her for a time."

The words spilled out of him, coming from a place within him he did not know, but Jasper felt the truth of them, could taste their veracity. Speaking his mind, his heart, like this to a relative stranger was an odd situation to be in, but with Lady Romeril acting as a gatekeeper, there was nothing for it but honesty.

"I..." Jasper sighed. "I love her so much, Lady Romeril, you must believe me. I would speak with her, if I may, and after that...well, if she does not want to see me again..."

Lady Romeril elegantly stepped aside, her wide skirts rustling.

Behind her, perhaps there all along…was Opal.

Jasper's stomach dropped. Right out of his body, onto the floor, leaving him with nothing but a gaping hole in his chest.

Opal.

Had she heard much of their conversation? Had she, in fact, heard all? Every word?

Jasper tried to think, but thinking was quite out of the question with Opal there. The children—where were they?

Lady Romeril smirked, as though she had played a very clever jest on the two of them. "I think I will leave the two of you to discuss things—though I expect a full report afterward, Mrs. de Petras."

She swept away in a flurry, and Jasper tried to maintain his calm demeanor, though it was nothing to the riot of confusion within his heart.

In a way, he felt as though he had already made his big speech declaring his love and affection for her, and now he felt off-kilter. As though all momentum had been taken from him, the wind out of his sails. What was he supposed to say now?

Opal stepped forward, cheeks darkening. "You were busy declaring your love for me, I believe."

Stepping forward, Jasper reached out his hands, desperate for her touch, desperate to pull Opal into his arms and feel her closeness, know she was with him, know she was safe.

Before he could, Opal put out a hand. "Speeches aside, and I admit yours was very pretty, I…I am not sure if I am ready for you to touch me again. Not after…not after meeting…"

Her voice trailed away into a painful whisper, then into complete silence. She looked truly heartbroken, and Jasper's heart broke in turn.

"My landlady… Jasper said haltingly, gaining confidence as he continued, "and I know that does not make everything better immediately. I know I cannot expect you to just trust me out of nowhere. I know I broke your trust by leaving all those years ago—but I don't just want to make it right, I want to make it better. I love you."

Opal's face turned white, and Jasper knew with certainty that Mrs. Norton's appearance at their home was the reason for Opal's disappearance.

"Your…your landlady?"

Jasper nodded and moved to the top step. To his great relief, Opal did not move away.

"Mrs. Norton owns a boarding house in the East End," explained Jasper quietly. "Do not ask me where, for I will never take you, 'tis no place for a lady. I paid her for the room and two meals a day the last few weeks, while I was ashore. That was all."

Hesitantly, Opal's eyes met his own. "And that was all?"

Jasper nodded. "I promise."

If he had hoped Opal would immediately rush into his arms and tell him all was forgotten and all was forgiven, Jasper was very much disappointed. Instead, she remained out of reach, her face pale and her lips twisted in indecision.

"I…I cannot trust you," Opal said quietly. "I—"

"Oh, Mrs. Norton, I know of the woman and a very respectable boarding house she manages," came Lady Romeril's voice.

Jasper blinked. He stepped across the threshold and saw Lady Romeril had disappeared into a room to the right—but the door itself was still open, and the woman was evidently listening.

He glared at the sliver of Lady Romeril he could see through the crack of the door, Admiral at her heels. Opal stepped forward smartly and shut the door in Lady Romeril's face.

She turned back to him. "Oh."

Jasper stepped toward her. "We are not a normal couple."

Opal laughed dryly. "We certainly are not!"

"But that is what I love about us," said Jasper urgently. "You and I, we are different from the rest of the world. You are the head of this family, but that does not mean you should have to do this all on your own. I want to support you—I love you."

A small smile crept across Opal's lips, and Jasper's heart soared.

"I want to be a better husband, a better father, so I never miss a moment again."

Opal's smile broadened, and when she spoke again, it was a shy sort of flirtation. "Does this mean you are asking me to marry you again?"

Jasper grinned. That was his Opal, the woman he had been captivated by all those years ago. She was still there, no part of her was misplaced.

Closing the gap between them, Jasper kissed her neck. "After what we've shared, we should definitely be married. Yes, please, marry me. Just don't make me beg."

Opal laughed as she offered up her lips, and as Jasper passionately pulled her into his arms and bestowed an ardent kiss upon her, he felt truly complete for the first time in seven years.

CHAPTER NINETEEN

May 26, 1794

OPAL SIGHED WITH happiness and wondered how she could have ever doubted it would end this way.

She should have trusted Jasper—and of course, he should have trusted her. But that seemed to be the way they worked. Always learning, having to adapt, finally able to find true love, the true happiness they should have had.

Opal sighed again with pleasure as she walked slowly up the aisle of the church. It had not mattered which one; the wedding had been organized hastily as it was, and the most important people in the world to her were already standing in the pews, watching her walk toward the man she loved.

There were the children. They had each been bought new clothes for such a day, and Micah was pulling at his collar most uncomfortably.

A snuffling sound echoed around the church, and Opal attempted not to roll her eyes. Of course, they had not been persuaded to leave Admiral at home.

Behind them was the Earl of Maltravers and his boy, James, who looked equally as uncomfortable in his cravat. Opal smiled at them. Friends to her husband, to be sure, but friends to the entire de Petras family. She would have to learn to depend on them, just as she was learning to depend once again on Jasper.

The other side of the church, the bride's side, was almost empty. Only Lady Romeril stood there with her husband and two boys. A rather knowing smile danced across her lips, and Opal made a note to ensure the woman remained her friend for life.

She knew far too much.

But Opal could not worry about such things for long, not as her gaze fell on the reason they were all here.

Jasper. He was attired most elegantly, a beaming smile on his face, and Opal's heart leapt.

There were few men, surely, in the world who could convince a woman to fall in love with them twice, but then Jasper de Petras was no typical man, and their courtship had been no less typical.

She loved him. Yes, they had suffered their fair share of troubles—but none of them truly mattered if they could be side by side.

"Dearly beloved," said the vicar as his meager congregation took their seats, "we are gathered here today to join this man with this woman…again."

Opal giggled, and she could not help it.

Well, it was all so strange, wasn't it? Like something out of a fairy story.

Jasper winked.

"Ahem. Yes," said the vicar rather severely. "I suppose you have the rings, we just need the vows. Do you, Opal de Petras…"

The vows rushed by in a haze. Opal could barely take them in, all her attention had been focused on the man before her who was holding her hands. Was that her pulse throbbing excitedly, or his?

"—pronounce you husband and wife," said the vicar sourly.

Opal knew it was not expected, knew that it was rather scandalous indeed, but she did not care. She had been apart from Jasper for four and twenty hours, and it was impossible to keep her away from him any longer.

Much to the surprise of all those present, and creating a few gasps that she was sure came from Lady Romeril, Opal leaned forward, pulled Jasper towards her by his justacorps, and kissed him hard on the mouth.

"Mother!"

"Well, really!"

Jasper, however, did not appear to mind. His hands had moved to her waist, holding her close, and it seemed an eternity until he released her, just as breathless as she was.

Opal smiled, a little shame-faced. "I know we should have waited until we left the church, but—"

"Let's never wait for anything ever again," said Jasper firmly. "Well, sir, is that all?"

The vicar blinked. "All? Well, yes, I suppose—"

"Marvelous," said Jasper brightly. "Good day to you."

He grasped Opal's hand, and her heart soared as they walked back down the aisle, once again husband and wife. It felt so right, as though the world had been off-kilter until this moment. Until they were together again as they should be.

"My dear Mrs. de Petras, I must have missed part of my invitation," said Lady Romeril who attempted to keep up with them as they walked to the church door. "I saw nothing about a reception."

"And that," Opal said politely but firmly, "is because you were not invited. Only the most important people in Society are invited for that."

She saw the Earl of Maltravers laughing in his seat as Lady Romeril's eyebrows rose.

"The most important people in Society?"

And so they were. Opal smiled as she looked at them, leaning against the shoulder of the man seated beside her on the sofa, his attention focused on the newspaper in his hands. Without looking away from the printed type, Jasper raised an arm, and Opal snuggled into him. Jasper's arm circled her waist, drawing her closer.

There was utter peace in the house, but not stillness. No stillness was entirely possible with three children about the place.

Coral was reading a book on the opposite sofa; one that Opal felt was a little advanced for her age, but then, who was she to stop someone from reading *The Romance of the Forest*?

By some miracle, one Opal did not yet understand and was loathe to investigate in case she broke the moment, Micah and Emerald were playing happily on the carpet between the two sofas.

The parlor had that nice lived-in look that Opal enjoyed so much. A few toys dotted about the place, an abandoned cup of tea either she or Jasper, she could not remember which, had likely put down while speaking to a child and then had forgotten about until it went cold.

The parlor of a family.

Opal smiled slowly, her heart soaring with love for them all. After last month's rather wild adventure to the Romerils' home, seeing the two boys there and the absolute mischief they got up to together, she was rather relieved to have separated her brood from Lady Romeril's.

Not that she would ever admit as much to the woman's face. That would not do.

Perhaps, though, the Romeril boys had had more of an effect on her three than she had expected. They had certainly been better behaved since they had returned home—or perhaps that was the calming presence of their father.

Perhaps, Opal thought wickedly, she should mention that to Lady Romeril the next time she saw her. Just a little hint. Payback after being forced to sit and listen to all her nonsense about her own boys.

Yet maybe not. Opal's smile did not disappear exactly, but it did falter a little. Poking at Lady Romeril was a dangerous pursuit at the best of times, and after what she had said at the church that morning…

Well, Lady Romeril had far too much ammunition for gossip

on the de Petras family. Opal did not like it, but then, there was nothing to be done about it. She would merely have to hope Lady Romeril's better instincts won the day, and she did not consider it worth her while to spread malicious gossip about the de Petras family.

A strange rustling sounded. Opal looked over at her husband to see that he was struggling to turn the page of his newspaper, now she had claimed his right hand.

Without saying a word, Opal raised her hand and helped him to turn the page. Jasper nodded without speaking, and his gaze immediately returned to the paper.

Was it possible to be this happy forever? Opal was sure it was rare, but if anyone was able to do it, then surely it would be them.

She smiled as her gaze flickered over to their eldest daughter. The girl turned a page, her attention utterly absorbed as she took in the adventures of Adeline and Theodore.

She was a serious thing, Opal thought wistfully. Perhaps far too serious for a girl her age, but then she had grown up in a rather strange family with very strange goings-on.

The longer she could remain a child, the better.

Opal glanced over and saw a wide, untamed yawn from Emerald. It was followed by another. She nudged Jasper.

"What?" he muttered, not looking away from the newspaper.

Opal nudged him again, and as he looked at her, slightly bewildered, she nodded her head toward their youngest, who was now unable to keep her mouth closed when she yawned.

Jasper smiled, a smile of such love and affection that Opal was not sure how she prevented herself from exploding with happiness. It was too much.

"Come on, little ones," said Jasper gently.

This time, both Coral and Micah looked outraged.

"I am not little!" said Coral haughtily.

"And neither am I," Micah said quickly. "Not as little as Emerald, anyway."

Emerald took a deep breath and was about to scream, Opal just knew it.

"Littler ones than me, I meant," said Jasper hastily. Emerald deflated and blinked at her father, who continued, "Come on, off upstairs. It is well past your bedtime, I do not know what your mother is about, letting you stay up like this."

Opal smiled indulgently. "You are in charge of bedtimes, my dear."

Jasper grinned. "Don't be ridiculous, I am not in charge of anything. Off you go, children."

As expected, Emerald rose immediately, but Micah scowled. "Five more minutes."

"Absolutely not," said Opal firmly. "Come on, off to bed you go."

"Goodnight, Mother," Coral said primly as she stepped forward to kiss her mother on the cheek.

Micah followed suit, begrudging as always when it came to showing affection, and Emerald threw her arms around her mother before giving Opal a rather disturbingly sticky kiss. How did children manage to be so sticky?

After bidding her good night, they each kissed their father's cheek as Opal watched with a beaming smile.

The door closed behind the children, and a different kind of silence fell in the parlor. Softer. More mature.

"Goodness," said Jasper with a sigh. "We are fortunate to have them, aren't we?"

"Yes," Opal said firmly. "And we are fortunate to have you."

Her husband pulled a face Opal knew well; it was the "I understand what you are saying, but I completely disagree with you" face. One she had seen often.

"On the scale of fortunate, I am at the top, far higher than I deserve to be," said Jasper frankly. "Though you wouldn't know it to hear the way Coral goes on. I heard her discussing with Cook how we could make economies in the kitchen, the cheeky thing."

Opal laughed. "Yes, I should really take Coral in hand about that. 'Tis simply not right, though in a few years I suppose it will be par for the course. She does get so silly around money."

Which still did not make sense to Opal.

Jasper had a rather strange expression on his face. "You know, I never did discover where all the money in your family came from. I know you are the heir, and we have it safely invested, and all of that…but it must have come from somewhere."

Opal smiled but said nothing. Well, she could not have expected Jasper to wish to stay ignorant forever. Really, it was only because he had become her misplaced husband for half their marriage that it had taken nigh on ten years for the question to be seriously raised.

"And you must have had siblings, though I admit I cannot recall any," continued Jasper, a light frown on his forehead. "What did they do, if you inherited the bulk of your family fortune?"

Opal's smile wavered, just ever so slightly, before she was able to smile brightly.

There was so much about her past, at least her family's past, that she had managed to keep from him. So many truths she had hidden, though not many lies she had told.

One day, perhaps, she would tell him. Tell him everything. But right now…well, he deserved to know something.

"Did…did you ever meet my brother?"

Opal's chest had tightened as she said the words, as though by speaking of him she could conjure him. *Heaven forbid.*

Jasper twisted slightly to look at her. "No. Why? You have a brother?"

Opal considered telling him everything. Everything that had befallen, everything she suspected, everything that may occur in the future.

But it was too soon, surely. They had only recently gained a new understanding, a better understanding of each other. The last thing she wanted was to frighten him, to overwhelm him with what sort of a life they could have if her brother…

She could not conceive of anyone else who may wish her harm—but until it was proven, that was a story that could wait. Perhaps for years. Perhaps she would never tell it.

"We had a...call it a misunderstanding," said Opal delicately. Well, that was all it started as, wasn't it? "My misunderstanding, I suppose, but it became an argument. Quite a vicious one. Perhaps he was the one that wrote..."

Jasper leaned closer. "Siblings argue all the time, look at our brood—but to send letters such as we received? Surely you do not believe he could have written such things?"

Opal sighed. "I hate to say it, but I believe he could. I never mentioned it, but while you were gone, I received a letter from him myself, inviting me to France. A rapprochement, he called it. I refused, Emerald was far too little for me to be going anywhere, but...well. I wonder now whether he was hoping to denounce me to the Revolutionaries."

Jasper's face was a picture of horror. "You cannot think that—"

"Not all families are full of love and laughter," Opal reminded him gently. This was why she had not mentioned it before, she had known he would take it this way. "Not all families are like us."

He laughed at that. "None of them are. But Opal, if you truly believe it was your brother ...what are we going to do about him?"

It was a good question. Opal had never liked to think such awful things of her brother, and the letter inviting her to France had not spoken of any ill-feeling. She had hoped it came from a place of forgiveness—not that she thought she needed much forgiveness—but as it was...

"I shall have to make inquiries, I think," she said slowly. "Discreet ones."

There was a tension in her husband's brow she did not like. "He has done nothing about my return, so I suppose his attempt failed, in the end. What happened, then? Between the two of you, for things to be so bad?"

"Oh, Pietro's bark was always worse than his bite."

"Opal de Petras, you're not going to tell me, are you?"

Opal smiled. "Remind me to tell you about him someday."

Jasper sighed theatrically. "You only say that to ensure that I stay, teasing me along with promises of future stories."

There was a smile dancing on his lips, and Opal knew he was only teasing, but her heart still gave a painful lurch.

"Well," she said brightly, "on the subject of making you stay…"

Though Opal had not been sure how she would broach the topic, Jasper gave her no chance to do so. His kiss was heated, tantalizing, promising what could happen later that evening, and Opal sank into it with pleasure.

"I made a promise to you," Jasper said quietly as the kiss ended. "You may have misplaced me, but I was always your husband."

Opal leaned forward, capturing his lips with hers, tasting the sweetness of his affection and the spice of his desire. Her tongue quested along his lips, and Jasper opened his mouth, allowing her entrance, and his hands on her waist pulled her closer.

She lost herself in the kiss, in the man she loved, in the passion they had missed for so long. Torn apart by lies, fear, confusion…now brought together by the return of affection.

And lust. Definitely lust.

Opal pushed him back, her breath jagged and her heart knowing they could not continue. "Not now—not here."

Jasper had a rather wild look in his eyes. "Why on earth not?"

"Jasper—the servants!"

Her husband gave a shrug that made Opal's body tingle with anticipation.

"They could come here any moment! No, you will have to learn to control yourself."

Jasper groaned, falling against the sofa with a desperate expression. "I never was very good at that."

She laughed, unable to help herself.

"You know, Jasper," said Opal coyly, "I hope your promise to always be there for me will hold true."

"Of course it will," Jasper said with a smile on his face. "And I will always be here for our three children."

Opal swallowed. "Four."

A terrified look came over Jasper's face, and he spoke so hurriedly that his words tripped over each other as they poured from his mouth. "Look—no, Opal, I told you before, I did not get up to anything while I was—you cannot think I would father then hide a child!"

He really did look quite distraught.

Opal smiled. "I know you did not get up to anything while you were away, but...you got up to something when you came back."

For a moment, Jasper merely stared, eyes uncomprehending, tension knitted in his brows. A few heartbeats passed. Opal said nothing, and did not move. Knew that in a moment, he would understand it all.

Then Jasper jumped from the sofa and laughed with such an astonished air, his eyes wide, that he looked a little unbalanced. "You are not."

"I am," said Opal with a growing smile.

"No!"

"Trust me," Opal said wryly, "after three, you know."

Jasper laughed again, grabbing her hands and pulling her up, dancing about the room, and Opal loved him for it.

"Another child!"

"Another little de Petras," said Opal with a laugh. "Yes."

Jasper kissed her hard, and Opal responded, pulling him close, feeling the desire grow in her. There would be plenty of time for discussing the arrival of their fourth child. First, a celebration. Her misplaced husband was home.

EPILOGUE

Coral

February 1, 1795

THE BABY WAS placed in Coral's arms without her asking for it, but that was no matter. Two other smaller siblings had arrived, and each time Coral had accepted that this screaming thing was now a part of the family.

Coral looked at the baby, the tall back of the sofa behind her, ensuring she was supported as she looked into the light blue eyes of the child.

"Aaah, there you are, Sapphire," said Mama, cooing at the baby as she sank gently next to Coral and stroked the newborn's cheek. "Mother's here."

Admiral sighed heavily in his sleep, turning over on the sofa opposite her. Coral looked at her mother, then back at the baby. *Sapphire. Well, it was as good a name as any,* Coral thought, *and it fitted with the rest of the family.* Only time would tell just how the baby herself would fit in.

"Such a pretty baby," sighed her father.

Coral looked up. Her papa was looking with such pride, such joy. She had rarely seen him so overcome with emotion—well. Sometimes when her mother had got stuck halfway on the stairs, unable to get up or unable to get down, her swollen stomach inhibiting her. But he had laughed at that.

Glancing at her brother on the other side of the sofa, Coral saw with a smile that he looked just as uninterested as she did. She caught his eye. Micah shrugged. It appeared the second de Petras child was just as indifferent about the arrival of the fourth as she was. Perhaps more. Micah had never spoken of it, not to her, but Coral had a suspicion he had wanted a brother.

But no, it was a girl. Sapphire de Petras.

Coral looked again at the baby, far heavier in her arms than she had imagined for such a small thing. Sapphire's little arms wriggled out of the blanket she was wrapped in, little fingers on one hand and the stub at her wrist on the other waving in the air, as though trying to catch Coral's nose.

Her mama had explained when Sapphire had first been presented to the de Petras children. "Sapphire's arm is a little different," she had said with a warm smile but tired eyes, "but she is healthy and happy and beautiful."

Coral had nodded. Everyone was a little different. Her fiery red hair did not match either of her siblings—or now, she supposed she should say, any of them.

"Look at that clever little thing," their mother said with a smile, watching her youngest's arms waving about.

Coral could not help but smile, too, seeing the love in her mama's face. Was this how she had looked at Coral when she had been the only little one?

"Isn't she perfect?"

Coral frowned at her father's question and looked more closely at the baby. Blue eyes, soft dander for hair that was dark in some lights and fair in others. She looked, in truth, much like Emerald had done when she had been born, and though she could not precisely recall what Micah had looked like at birth, Coral was almost certain he had looked the same.

"She's a baby," Coral said slowly. "And all babies look the same."

Her father laughed as her mama said, "No they don't! You all looked completely different, I promise you."

Coral's gaze slipped to her brother, who shrugged again and rose from the sofa.

If only she could follow him.

Coral looked at her mother. "Are you going to have another baby?"

"Absolutely not," said her mother firmly, at the same time her father said, "Perhaps."

Coral watched, fascinated as her parents looked at each other. There was a strange expression on her father's face, one she could not understand. Her mother was easier to read.

Her mama laughed. "Absolutely not! Four is quite enough, thank you. If you want another one, you are going to have to learn to carry one yourself!"

A flush rose in Coral's cheeks as she tried not to think about what her parents must have done to create the child now in her arms. Best not to think about it.

Sapphire wriggled most uncomfortably. Her eyes were wide open, and Coral found a smile crept over her face. She was a pretty child.

"Little Sapphire," Coral whispered.

"You know, I think I should name the next one," said her papa grandly, seating himself on the sofa opposite his wife and daughters. "No more of these precious stones."

Coral smiled as she watched her parents chatter. They were happy—such a rare state of affairs these last few years, she was eager to enjoy it while she could. Her mother had been so unhappy for so long, that it was hard to remember what her mother's happiness looked like. It made one decide never to marry at all.

If the point was to be happy, Coral had often wondered, then why were so many married people miserable? It did not make any sense…

"Well, a compromise is reached," said her papa, moving over

to their sofa and kissing his wife on the head. "The moment I can work out how to bear the pains of labor for you, we'll have triplets."

Their laughter rang out in the room as Coral smiled. "I am glad you are back, Papa."

"I should think so, too," he said with a twinkle in his eyes.

"Though I suppose you are another mouth to feed," Coral said quietly.

"You always worry about money," grumbled Micah from behind her.

"No, I don't," snapped Coral, her temper rising rapidly. *What was it about brothers that made them so entirely irritating?*

"Coral, dear, you do know it was your mother who had most of the money when we married?" pointed out their father mildly.

Coral sniffed but did not say anything.

And she was the eldest daughter, the eldest female de Petras. She would inherit whatever was left after her parents raised them all.

"I will have you know, I will never worry about money again," said Coral sharply to the brother she could not see. "When I marry, it will be to a very wealthy man."

"Are you getting married?" Emerald asked from behind the sofa.

Heat seared Coral's cheeks. "Not *now.*"

"Goodness, I am not sure I could cope with any of you girls leaving home yet," said their father mildly. "Give me a few more years!"

Coral smiled at her father's jest. "I am serious."

"Oh, Coral, you cannot just decide to marry for money," Opal teased. "You are far too much of a romantic."

"Oh yes, I can. When I marry, it will not be for love. That I promise you. I will never marry for love."

Discover whether Coral is able to hold to her convictions in…The Impoverished Dowry…Book 2 of THE DE PETRAS SAGA.

About Emily E K Murdoch

If you love falling in love, then you've come to the right place.

I am a historian and writer and have a varied career to date: from examining medieval manuscripts to designing museum exhibitions, to working as a researcher for the BBC to working for the National Trust.

My books range from England 1050 to Texas 1848, and I can't wait for you to fall in love with my heroes and heroines!

Follow me on twitter and instagram @emilyekmurdoch, find me on facebook at facebook.com/theemilyekmurdoch, and read my blog at www.emilyekmurdoch.com.

www.ingramcontent.com/pod-product-compliance
Lightning Source LLC
Chambersburg PA
CBHW070952190726
48292CB00004B/1430